A DESPERATE SEARCH
FOR LASTING PEACE

When the American Embassy closed in
Peking, diplomat Malcolm MacNeil had
no choice but to settle his family in the
United States. There he would write and
lecture and there his beautiful White-
Russian wife and two China-born children
would find the security and humanity for
which his whole life had been a search.

Many things about his new home confused and disturbed him—but what hurt
most deeply was the atmosphere of
distrust, misunderstanding and hostility
which, even in America, his family seemed
powerless to escape.

ALL UNDER HEAVEN
was originally published by The John Day Company.

Books by Pearl S. Buck

A Bridge for Passing
All Under Heaven
The Angry Wife
Come, My Beloved
Command the Morning
Death in the Castle
Dragon Seed
The Exile
Fighting Angel
The Goddess Abides
God's Men
The Good Earth
Hearts Come Home and Other Stories
The Hidden Flower
Imperial Woman
Kinfolk
Letter from Peking
The Living Reed
The Long Love
Mandala
The Mother
My Several Worlds
The New Year
Pavilion of Women
Peony
Portrait of a Marriage
The Three Daughters of Madame Llang
The Time is Noon
The Townsman
Voices in the House

Published by POCKET BOOKS

Pearl S. Buck

ALL
UNDER
HEAVEN

PUBLISHED BY POCKET BOOKS NEW YORK

ALL UNDER HEAVEN

John Day edition published 1973

POCKET BOOK edition published December, 1974

L

Standard Book Number: 671-78698-9.
Library of Congress Catalog Card Number: 72-7285.

Front cover illustration by Jim Avati.

Printed in the U.S.A.

I

"THERE IT IS—that glorious skyline—the greatest in the world!"

Malcolm MacNeil, excited, exultant, spoke to his wife, Nadya. She clung to his arm as they stood by the rail of the upper deck. The ship was nearing New York. The east wind was blowing sharply across the Atlantic and Nadya's profile was all but lost in her flying hair, pale yellow, straight and fine. She had cut it shoulder length only yesterday and he did not know when he could forgive her for it. He had supposed, when she said that she was going to the ship's beauty shop, that she would have only her usual shampoo. She had never learned to wash her own hair—in Peking the amah had done it—and he was proud enough of the heavy mass of it so that he allowed her the small luxury even after they had left Hong Kong. But to come back with it cut off! He looked away from her now, determined not to say more than he had said yesterday when she had flung the shorn bright stuff into his hands.

"Can you see the shape of the city?" he asked.

"I see it," Nadya replied.

She spoke with a Russian accent and in Peking it had been charming, distinguished among the many other accents. How would it sound in America? He had never spoken his anxieties about her in America and he had made up his mind that he never would. Instead, he would be merely watchful, taking each incident as it came. He would explain to his countrymen over and over again, as often as necessary, that she was White Russian, not Red Russian, and there was the whole difference of the modern world between the two.

Years ago her parents had escaped with her from Russia. They had stolen away in the night from their home and their hereditary lands near Moscow. They were friends of the Czar and somewhere or other perhaps even blood relations, but that Nadya did not know. She could barely remember the flight to Manchuria, for she had been only five, and her parents were still young. She had grown up in Harbin. When Japan seized Manchuria the family escaped again, this time to Peking.

"But they are castles," Nadya now said, gazing at the famous skyline of New York. "And you, Malcolm, did never tell me that in America are castles!"

She turned her delicate profile to him and he looked into her large and accusing blue eyes.

"You expect me to tell you everything at once," he replied. "Besides, they are not castles. They are skyscrapers."

"There is difference?" she inquired.

"Vast," he replied.

They had risen early so that they could see the city

loom from the mists of spring. No one was on the deck yet except themselves, though toward the stern he could see many heads below, some in kerchiefs. Steerage passengers were still immigrants, he supposed, since Nadya had wanted to come by way of Europe, but he was no immigrant. He was an American coming home, richer by Nadya and the two children, after twenty-five years in diplomatic service in China. Twenty-five years of a career that he had supposed would be life-long! It did not bear thinking about. Simply, it had become impossible to live in Peking, the city they loved, and where he had first found Nadya. She had then been a slender, brilliant creature already helping to support her mother by teaching languages in a Chinese university. Her father, who had died in an epidemic of bubonic plague, had been more than the usual Russian nobleman. He had been a scholar, and in Peking he had done scholar's work at last, an opportunity not to be found in the crude border towns of Manchuria. Thus Nadya had been spared the tragedy of most White Russian daughters of noble families. She had not been compelled to be a dancer in a café nor had she become the concubine of a fat old Chinese warlord.

The year her mother died of the lingering disease of sprue Malcolm had married the lovely girl. They had been entirely happy in Peking, so happy that under another circumstance he might have resigned from the service when the embassy was closed and have tried to stay. But the terror in Nadya's face when he suggested this had been enough to prevent him. She had clutched her breast in the instinctive dramatic gesture that was natural to her.

"The Communists will kill me!" she gasped.

He saw in her eyes memories her parents had put there when they fled their country carrying her with them.

"This is China, not Russia, Nadya." So he had reminded her.

"Oh, no, Malcolm," she had insisted. "Bolsheviki are ever the same, only now called Communists, but still the same. They will destroy me, for I am the daughter of my father and my mother."

"You are my wife now," he had reminded her. "And I am American."

"Then let us go to America," she had cried eagerly.

He felt her suddenly shiver now as her body pressed against his own, and he put his hand on her hands clasped over his arm.

"You are cold," he exclaimed.

"Excited only," she said. She flashed him her quick and brilliant smile and he was silent. He had learned not to adjure her to be calm. She was strung on golden wires, sensitive as the high strings of a harp, and she could not more help responding to every touch and change. He had learned to make his own natural calm protect her changefulness. Thus now he kept his large quiet hand over her small clasped ones. They were cold, indeed, but his hand was warm. His steady bloodstream did not alter, whatever happened. Heredity, a placid childhood, his college major in philosophy, the years in China, whatever it might be, had early infused his being with the habit of peace. He was not afraid of his own country. It was good to come home.

In the hotel rooms in New York, a few hours later, he considered his family thoughtfully while the unpacking went on. He took no part in it, for it was good for the children and especially for Nadya to need be busy about small affairs. He discerned fright in her pure, bright smile and in the electric clarity of her blue eyes.

The two children, Peter and Lise, at thirteen and eleven, were young enough merely to be excited. At least he hoped so. They were both more like Nadya than like him, and he wondered sometimes, half amused, if this meant she was the stronger. Meanwhile the children were dividing the drawers of a bureau in amiable mood.

"Ta Ko," Lise said in Chinese to her brother, "you will take the two upper drawers and I the two lower ones, since you are the taller."

"Such a good Mei Mei!" Nadya cried. Her natural ardor compelled her to kiss her daughter's cheek and then, lest her son feel himself neglected, she kissed also the shining swirl of his crown.

Malcolm took the pipe from his mouth. "I suppose," he said in his easy drawl, "that since we are in America and are Americans, we had better stop using the Chinese names. Ta Ko will now become Peter and Mei Mei will be Lise."

"Must we do so?" Nadya inquired. She paused with a pile of her fine silk undergarments, embroidered by nuns in a Peking convent.

"Cannot I be called Mei Mei when no one is with us?" Lise asked.

"I wish to be called Peter," her brother said firmly.

Malcolm smiled. A handsome family, his! Just now he supposed they were overwrought. He must be careful to find exactly the right beginning for this new life. Nadya had brought sensitive blood to join his phlegm, and yet she had a substratum of good sense, partly heredity, partly the necessity of her hard early years.

"We don't need to decide everything at once," he replied. "I merely make a suggestion. We will accommodate ourselves."

Nadya hung up a cloud of rose tulle, attached to a

narrow bodice. "And what happens to us now, Malcolm?" she asked. "We will not stay in New York, no?"

"We will stay a few days," he said in the lazy manner he had cultivated when he discovered that underneath her lovely face Nadya concealed a terror of change. That escape from death by mob, in Russia, when she was too small, he would have said, to remember anything, had nevertheless left its shadows. She could not remember, she said she could not, and yet when confronted with the vast black turmoil of the sea at night she had murmured once that it made her remember something, what she did not know, a feeling more than a shape. And a mob, oh, a mob of human faces had the utmost horror for her. Even on feast days in Peking, when the mobs of people were laughing and pushing and overflowing with kindliness, she could not look at them. On such days she barred the compound gate, and even so the sound of the roar of human voices pouring over the walls compelled her into the house and she closed the windows and doors.

"It gives me always such a feeling!"

It was her only explanation. But he supposed the feeling was all that remained of the memory of the night when her father's own serfs had driven them away from the ancestral home. Well, and thank God, there was no more need for such fears now. When they had found the place they wanted to live and make their home, the shadows would flee away. Years of solid life waited for them. He had married a little late—he was now already fifty and Nadya was nearly fifteen years his junior—but he was young yet and looked far younger than he was. Before he was old the children would be grown and Nadya would be safe with them. His task now was to make sound roots for them all, to choose the place from which they need never move again. He wished his parents were alive. They had died years ago, but he had his two sisters, both married and with families, both younger than he. And he had cousins, he supposed, whom he had not seen or seen so long ago that he had forgotten them, but now he must look them all up for the sake of his children. He must become a sort of patriarch, elder uncle, and so on, in the sound Chinese fashion, recognizing the need of the human creature to be enfolded and surrounded by its kind. He must give his own children this security, which Nadya could not give them.

"Malcolm, how is it you do not answer my question to you?" Nadya was saying.

"My love, did you ask me a question?" he inquired mildly.

"I askéd you," Nadya said, making always two distinct syllables of the word, "what do we do in New York?"

He took his pipe out of his mouth. "There is more to do here than in any city in the world—theaters, museums, concerts, shops—you will want to buy some clothes for yourself and the children."

"I wish to buy things for myself," Peter put in.

"For myself," Lise chanted. "I wish to buy an American walking doll. A girl on the ship told me there are such dolls."

They both spoke English like European children, or English children, he thought. Ah well, public school would change that!

"You may each choose for yourselves," he told them.

"I think I will not buy clothes at once," Nadya said prudently.

She was careful with money, far more careful than she needed to be, he thought, smiling at her. His father had left him a small inheritance and he had been able to save. The inflation that had driven the Chinese people to despair had been kind to American dollars.

Nevertheless, prudence was wise. They would want to buy a house. He took out his watch. "As soon as you have settled yourselves, we will get some lunch and then take a walk and see the town. This will give us the opportunity to choose what we shall do first."

Nadya replied to this with enthusiasm. "Ah, how I am hungry!"

He was accustomed to the brilliant northern sunshine of Peking shining down upon yellow-tiled imperial palaces and upon the royal blue of temple roofs. White walls and scarlet dyes and the solid old blue of peasant cotton had sharpened the color contrast in those wide and dusty streets. This city of New York was brilliant in a style entirely its own. In spite of his many years in Peking and his profound and unshakable love for that city, his feelings now as he walked the narrow, glittering streets of the modern New York were of wonder. The mellow toleration that was the natural atmosphere of his spirit was infused with sharp pride. He had not been in New York for more than twenty years. In those years, while he had been living in calm Asian happiness, this city had grown to a scintillating maturity. Or was it still young? The clean spring air made it difficult to decide. There was chill enough in the sea wind so that beautiful young women walked the streets holding their furs to their throats, their cheeks pink. Lips, of course, were scarlet and that was something new. Twenty years ago not every American woman painted her lips. But he liked it. Chinese women had painted themselves thus for centuries and the color added vitality to any woman. Why not? He liked to see his Nadya's beautiful mouth brighten the golden pallor of her face and hair. And the women, the women suited the brightness of this gem of a city, this city of shining windows and soaring spires. He liked the swift, controlled movement in the streets, the cabs and cars dashing headlong and then like tamed beasts stopping at the signal of the red light. This was the very essence of the modern, both speed and control.

"So like to tigers crouching," Nadya murmured anxiously.

They were at a corner, waiting to cross the street and the light changed. Nadya had hesitated, her eyes on the cabs couchants.

"Come, Mamá!" Peter cried, frantic at delay. "It is the green light!"

They took hands and hurried across the street and Malcolm was conscious of smiles and glances. He laughed.

"I have a family of greenhorns," he declared when they were across. "Look, my infants, it is not necessary to reach the opposite side in one moment of time. We are allowed to walk like reasonable creatures. We are not asked to race others who walk."

He spoke in Chinese—they all spoke Chinese as easily as English, and when he wished to impress without scolding, instinctively he dropped into the kindly tongue.

"Yes, Malcolm," Nadya said for the children, "but we must learn day by day such things. This is the first day."

They stopped a few minutes later to wonder at a shop window on Fifth Avenue, and looking at Nadya, Malcolm saw tears pouring down her cheeks. He was not troubled. Nadya had the Russian need to weep and she did so easily and often. At first this melting had wracked his heart. Now he merely took her hand.

"It is wonderful to see not a beggar," Nadya sobbed. "Not one, Malcolm! Where are they? Can it be true that here is not one beggar?"

"Since you do not see them, I suppose there are none," he replied reasonably.

People were looking at them but he outstared them, his gray eyes suddenly hard. If Nadya wished to weep she could weep and none must laugh at her.

"Now," she said. She wiped her eyes and laughed suddenly. "I am crying because I need not to see hungry people any more. Oh, I do love America already!"

"Since you feel happy," he replied, "let us go into Radio City and see the show. I have heard it is amusing."

All Chinese who visited New York went first and if possible daily to Radio City. When they returned to Peking they told and retold its delights until everyone dreamed of Radio City. He piloted them into the vast building, crowded with people released from work and worry—the people's palace, he thought, thick carpets under the feet, immense balconies, music straining through the distance, lackeys in uniform waiting to serve. There was no place like it, surely, anywhere else in the world and it was as much his as anyone's, and so he supposed each person felt as he came through the mighty doors. The price of a ticket seemed little enough to admit one into such magnificence.

"Reserved seats, please," he said, and with these small passports in his hand he followed an usher into a box facing the enormous stage. Magic and more magic! He was torn between his own desire to miss nothing and yet to share in every wonder on the faces of his wife and children.

"How it is done so smooth, so easy," Nadya whispered. The orchestral stage, itself as big as a railroad platform, was rising up out of lower darkness. The full lights emblazoned musicians, all smiling, all immaculate, and music burst from them together in a furious chorus of instruments. But Nadya put her hands to her ears in sudden pain. "Oh, too fast!" she hissed at them. "Oh, what do they do?"

"Mamá, what is the matter?" Lise inquired aloud.

Over the low barriers people in the other boxes were looking at them.

"It is Tchaikovsky," Nadya complained, her hands still at her ears. "Yes, but something they do, it is like a whipping to the music! How can they so?"

She dropped her hands and clenched them in her lap and Malcolm put out his hand and covered them. The music was the finale of a concerto, twisted into a syncopated, agonizing spiral of sound. Suddenly it ended, incomplete. The musicians sank again into their depths, a clown ran across the stage, and Nadya forgot. She laughed and the children laughed with her. A little dog rode out on a high-wheeled bicycle and they were beside themselves with joy. Trained seals elbowed their way from behind the curtains and a smart ringmaster snapped his commands.

"Oh, Malcolm," Nadya cried in ecstasy, "please to see the little shining seal, the small creature clapping for himself with his fins! The adorable! I would like to have him for my own."

"Mamá, couldn't we have a seal?" Lise asked.

"It is the dog I wish," Peter said.

Malcolm did not reply. He was accustomed to their extremes, and they knew well enough that neither seal nor dog could be had. The desire to own, to press to their bosoms, was mere overflow of ardent enjoyment.

When they came out of the people's palace the streets were glittering with lights and they walked back arm in arm to the hotel, oblivious to the barrier they made, thus linked, to other pedestrians. Even Malcolm felt himself bemused. All in all, it had been royal entertainment, shallow but gay and refreshing. He had seen enough of human sorrow for the rest of his life. His years in China had been filled with the troubles of revolution and war. For two hours and a half he had forgotten it all. Such a thing had not happened to him since he was a college boy in Harvard.

It was midnight and he could not sleep. The unfamiliar noises of the street seemed never to end and he got up out of bed and went to the open window. Noises there had been in the Peking streets, too, and they had floated over the compound walls and into the open windows of the spreading Chinese house that had been their home. He had loved the closeness to earth and heaven of its vast rooms and small courtyards. The house had no cellars—it was built solid to the ground—and to step out of a room meant to have one's feet on the earth and to look up meant to see the wideness of heaven. Now, suspended between, he looked eighteen stories down into canyoned streets, and ten stories up into a strip of starlit sky. He felt a strange loneliness in this, the most crowded city in the world, but it was not the city that made him lonely. That quality was common to all cities. What he felt was a peculiar emotion, the loneliness of the exile returned.

Would his country welcome him and his family? He remembered well enough the years of his youth, those pleasant years in a small town where his father was the editor of the local newspaper, the most famous man, a small fame at that, not reaching very far. He had gone to school with boys whom he liked and then he had forgotten them because he went away to college and they did not. When he came back the home town seemed tight and small and he discerned a strange, proud, contemptuous jealousy among his friends. Would he or would he not, they seemed to inquire, never in words, but in reserved manners and quiet eyes or in too boisterous greetings, this depending upon their natures, would he or would he not be different, now that he had been east to a big college?

He had not stayed to answer their question. It was not worth answering. His father had been the big frog in the little pond, but he preferred to find a big pond where at first he might be small but where he could grow to his own size, a difficult thing, perhaps, in a country where levels were all fluid and anybody might be President—if he could. He had never quite found himself in the big pond, however. He was, he supposed, too much the intellectual, which his father had been, too, but had been clever enough to conceal.

"The secret of living in a democracy," his father had once told him, "is to find out what the other fellow is like and then be as like him as you decently can."

Cynical words, and he had not accepted them. He preferred merely to go away. Nevertheless, it was not until he had been sent to Peking as a young vice-consul that he had found a country where he could be himself. In China the intellectual was the aristocrat and had been for centuries, and in Peking, where was the essence of all that was Chinese, he had found his friends. It was no disgrace there for a man of business to pursue the arts and the graces of the mind.

Yet it was Nadya who had first pointed out to him the danger of peace for the intellectual, even in Peking. Years before the final disaster she had shivered at the arrogance, the self-satisfaction, of the Chinese intellectuals. He well remembered the night when they had dined with that king of them all, Dr. Meng Liang, an intellectual of the West as well of the East. The brilliant evening shone intact in his memory. Pure intelligence had informed the conversation, and acute instinct, quick intuition, deep learning, detached emotion, had provided such entertainment as perhaps he would never find again. But Nadya, perfectly comprehending and wholly enjoying, had come home sad, although the Peking night had been clear, unearthly in silence and beauty.

"It touches me at the heart," she had said when he inquired of her sadness. She had gone on to explain. "They do not know what they do, these men and women of shining minds. They think of everything in the universe and do not feel their own danger."

"Danger?" He had repeated the word stupidly. At that time he had known so little.

"In Russia so it was, also," Nadya said. "I remember my dear little father telling me, 'Ah, Nadya,' he said many times, 'if only we had known in time, we intellectuals, we who had the treasures of learning! If only we had not worn our learning as jewels for our own decoration and our own joy!'"

He had still been stupid. "What did he mean, Nadya?" This had been his stupid question.

"Oh, Malcolm, how can you not understand?" she had cried at him. "The poor and the ignorant are patient, they will respect and worship those who know more than they do, who possess the secrets, they think, that will take away poverty and pain and sickness and death. But when in Russia they saw those who had the secrets using them only for their own good, then they rose up in such wrath that we were killed. Oh, thousands upon those thousands of us died because we did not know our dangers soon enough."

He had comforted her. "It will be different in China. Here men of learning have always been revered. Centuries cannot be quickly changed, Nadya. It does not happen so."

Ah, he thought, leaning out of the window in New York, there was where he had been wrong! It had happened so, and very quickly. Never while his mind lived would he forget the day when the peasants took over the city of Peking, the angry, triumphant, ignorant peasants, led by an angry master peasant. The foundations of Chinese society, so carefully laid since the times of Confucius, five hundred years before Christ, were torn away and who would rebuild them again—and when?

These were questions without answer, and he had faced them before and knew that there was no answer. He went away from the window and walked noiselessly into the next room to look at his children. They were asleep in the narrow hotel beds, his son lying half outside the blankets, and his daughter curled beneath them in a cocoon. The strange new sounds of the city had not troubled them. They felt safe with their parents near and they had fallen asleep. He adjusted the blankets and then stood looking at them. What responsibility was his! For the first time since their birth, he half regretted that he had brought them into the world. He was responsible for them and he alone. Nadya was as helpless, too, as a child in this land she did not know. It was he who must choose and plan. As soon as he had made his report in Washington he must devote himself to his family. He would resign from the service, that much he must do. He had no heart for fresh assignments in some country foreign to him. It was time to put down roots for his children to feed upon and grow.

He felt suddenly cold and he shivered and crept back to bed and covered himself. Some small town, he thought drowsily, some comfortable little place where the windows shone at night with lamplight, a church spire, a school, a general store. As he drifted into sleep, the memories came welling up into his half-conscious mind. He must find such a place as soon as he had reported to Washington and was released to his own country.

The atmosphere of the important office in Washington was calm. The bustle of the lower offices had been disturbing as Malcolm was hurried through them. Did they know what they were doing here? He had often wondered, in Peking. Now after long waits and sudden movement he was ushered into this top office where a quiet, long-legged man with a haggard face stood looking out of a large window upon the Lincoln Memorial and the early-blooming cherry trees.

He turned when Malcolm came in and gave him a mild handshake. "I am glad to see you again, MacNeil," he said as though it were only yesterday that they had parted. "And I hope," he went on with a slight smile as they sat down in comfortably worn leather chairs, "to change your mind about resigning. We need good Scots brains like yours."

"Thank you, sir," Malcolm said. "I'm afraid I can't change. I have certain personal responsibilities."

The distinguished man filled his pipe. "We all have those, and we learn to manage. The times are too big for any of us."

"With that I agree, sir," Malcolm said.

"I suppose you *are* a Scot—with that name?" his superior inquired. "A stupid question, doubtless!"

"My great-grandfather came from Scotland," Malcolm replied.

"Canny of him," the tall man murmured.

"I think so."

The conversation languished a moment while the tall man drew hard on his pipe. His manner changed abruptly. "Well, MacNeil, how much of it could we have helped over there in China?"

Malcolm replied with caution. "One reason I wanted to resign, sir, was so that I could speak my mind freely. I imagine, or perhaps I know, that my point of view will be the unpopular one and perhaps even in some time not too far off the dangerous one."

His superior took his pipe out of his mouth and smiled a slight, sad smile. "We are not as far gone as that, MacNeil."

To this Malcolm did not reply.

"What is this dangerous point of view?" his superior asked after a waited silence.

"I believe in history, sir," Malcolm said. His voice was steady, and his gray eyes were fixed upon that long, sensitive face opposite him. They met the shrewd blue eyes.

"That is to say, you believe in cause and effect."

"Entirely."

The tall man knocked the ash out of his pipe. "Then you believe that what has happened in China was inevitable."

"Given what had gone before in China—and the United States, sir."

The tall man sighed. "Well, let's get to the bottom of this——"

It was twilight when the bottom was reached. The two men were exhausted and each saw it in the other's face.

"Therefore I wish to resign, sir," Malcolm said finally. "This is why I will not change my mind. What has been done has been done. We can only dree our weird, as my old grandmother used to say. Nothing that I can do will change the course of events in the least iota."

"May it not be your duty, nevertheless, to try? There was a boy who put his finger in a hole in a dike and thereby saved a nation."

"The dike has broken," Malcolm said. "I am running for my life."

"I wish I could run for mine," the tall man said. Under his bristling eyebrows his deep-set eyes shone with deadly humor, and his thin face looked like a laughing skull.

Malcolm put out his hand. "Goodbye, sir. We may not meet again."

"You aren't leaving the country, I hope?" The long pale hand reached out and grasped the strong brown hand, darkened by Chinese sun.

"On the contrary, I shall bury myself in my country and for the rest of my life."

"You'll get tired of being buried."

"Perhaps I should have said lose myself in my country," Malcolm said. He shuffled into his topcoat, Chinese fashion, and reached for his soft felt hat. "I am going to lead the life of an ordinary man, and see what it feels like. I want my children to go to public school and grow up plain Americans. My wife is going to be a mere housewife."

"You'll find no excitement in that," the tall man said. He stood with his hands clasped in front of him and rocked back and forth on his heels.

"We've had enough excitement for our lifetime," Malcolm said. "All we want is peace."

A sharp, strange look flitted over the drawn face. "Ah," the tall man said, "That's all the world wants, I daresay."

Out again in the twilight of early spring Malcolm felt sorry for the man who was no longer his superior. The burdens of many accusations lay on those bent shoulders, and angry, ignorant voices had shouted against the sensitive, intelligent mind that shone so clearly in the sad eyes. How long did it take to dull the pain of such blows? He had once seen in Peking a young teacher accused of being a Communist. He had been arrested, stripped naked, and beaten to death in the streets by secret police of a desperate regime. After a while, not very long, it had been obvious that the young man felt no more pain. He was not unconscious, he still held up his head, he still shouted his innocence, but he felt no more pain. It was some time before he died, perhaps as long as half an hour.

"I am done with all that," Malcolm told himself abruptly.

If ever he could be done with it! Memories clung like leeches, sucking the life out of present joy. The evening in Washington was beautiful. A mist rose from the Potomac and the setting sun filtered through it, softened and quieting. Government workers stood at street corners waiting for buses, mild-eyed at the end of day. Little homes waited for them, small new houses crowded together in the hurry of the sudden growth of a nation. The city had become the power center of a changed world, but the workers did not know it. Each fulfilled his duty and went home at night to sleep. If he too could be as ignorant, as innocent, Malcolm thought as he strode along the sidewalk, how pleasant life could be! But could ignorance now be innocent? Too late for such questions!

Yet where could he go for escape from them? Two hundred years ago his ancestors had come from Scotland to this new country. They had gone to Virginia and had settled in the wilds of the Shenandoah Valley. His first ancestors had bought miles of timbered land and had laid the foundations of a fortune for generations to enjoy. The timber was felled and the land was made into fields and cattle grazed by the thousands upon the hillsides. Black slaves gave their lives and their laughter to the land, to the planting of orchards and to the making of a great mansion. Thomas Jefferson was the friend of Edgar MacNeil, and in the huge mansion there had been a library designed by Jefferson for his friend. But Edgar MacNeil had insisted upon a central hall and then a wide, winding stair, which Jefferson had protested. He had just torn the stairs out of his own great house at Monticello. Edgar MacNeil had been stubborn, nevertheless, and Jefferson had yielded and had presented gifts to his friend—a clock, a weathervane, a music rack like his own. The MacNeil mansion had descended from elder son to elder son until a generation ago a horseracing, speculating heir had ruined the family, had sold the house and land to pay his debts. He had then hung himself in the deserted barn. Out of that ruin Malcolm's father had salvaged his own youth and gone west.

The old house was for sale again now and Malcolm's sister, Corinne, wrote to tell him so. He had found the letter waiting for him at the hotel in Washington and had read it, wondering if he wished to restore the family to its ancestral seat.

"If you do," Corinne wrote, "I believe you can get it cheaply. It is in shocking repair. The great trees in the avenue have been cut down. I can't think why, unless for money. It will take some money to put it back into what it was, but perhaps you have it. We haven't. Anyway, the house always went to the son. Susanna and I"—Susanna was his younger sister—"have often talked about it. We agree that we could never feel at home in it."

The letter was in his pocket now. Did he wish to return to something already history or did he wish to pioneer, as his father had done? At any rate, he thought, swinging upward in the hotel elevator, a sensation so long strange to him that he felt giddy, it would do no harm to take Nadya and the children back to see the old mansion, and let the decision shape itself from their mingling emotions. On the tenth floor he got out and walked down the carpeted corridor to their rooms. The distant sound of hearty singing crept from under the door. Peter and Lise and Nadya were singing. She had taught them many songs, French, German, Chinese, and the Russian songs of her childhood. They were singing a Russian song now.

He opened the door impetuously, caution afire upon his lips. "Nadya!"

Their voices stopped. He saw three laughing faces turn toward him, and caution retreated. He had been about to cry, "Not Russian, for God's sake!" but he did not. No, he would not put fear into them. Here, at least, they must live free of fear.

He closed the door and flung off his coat. "I could hear you all the way down the corridor—perfect harmony! Some day we must exploit these kids of ours, Nadya. Meanwhile, are you hungry?"

"Ah, ha!" Nadya laughed aloud. "We are so hungry we are singing to forget it. We have planned what we shall eat. I will eat chicken."

"I will eat the fresh eggs in an omelette," Lise said. "I never knew how fresh eggs were before. Here no eggs are floating, I think."

This was her child's memory of eggs in Chinese markets, none to be bought unless first tested in water. Those than sank could be eaten, those that floated not.

"Steak, please, Father," Peter said.

Downstairs in the dining room he read Corinne's letter again, this time aloud while they waited for food. They listened intently, three blond heads leaning toward him, blue eyes fixed upon his face. The mansion was not strange to them. Far away in Peking he had taken pains to tell them all he knew about his country and his family. Thus they knew how Edgar MacNeil had left Scotland and how he had bought land unseen and found it far better than he had imagined it could be, the trees thicker than he could encompass in his arms, and the earth beneath his feet deep with the loam of silent centuries. They knew how many rooms the mansion had and how the pillared portico looked over the valley and the mountains beyond. They knew how it had been lost in the last generation and how the family had mourned the loss of the house more than the death of the man who had lost it, and how the widow and the children had taken their possessions and gone away, a thousand miles, so they need never see strangers in their home. Malcolm, their father, had gone back once to see it when he was grown. Decay had already begun. Strangers had not loved the house, and the war had freed the slaves and the land was in weeds.

"We should go to see it," Nadya now said gravely.

So during the meal they planned, and next day Malcolm drove them southward in a new car he had bought, an excitement in itself for the children had seldom ridden in an automobile, a vehicle they had thought in Peking belonged only to generals and presidents and officials, while Nadya had enjoyed her private ricksha.

"How smooth," Lise said, "how smooth goes the road beneath our wheels, how green are the hills and how blue is the sky!"

"She is happy," Nadya said tenderly. "I think we shall all be happy here in America, Malcolm, and we are so lucky there is this country to be ours."

Peter was silent. In the small mirror Malcolm looked at his son on the back seat and saw a face of perfect peace. Peter was gazing out of the window, seeing everything. He also was happy, and indeed happiness shone upon the countryside. He felt it himself, his heart lifted, and old burdens rolled away. He could forget the darkness of the storm over China. He had faithfully fulfilled his duty there, he had earnestly done his best, and it had not been enough. The vast discontent, the deep anger of a mighty people aroused beyond control, would roar still higher to heaven, and nothing and no one could stay the flames. The fires must burn out over yonder, and all that he could hope and pray for was that they did not spread across the oceans and the continents to inflame the world. He had withdrawn himself and his own as far as he could, and here, if anywhere, was safety, not only of retreat but of strength. He thanked God that he was a citizen of the strongest nation in the world.

"And why do you set your jaw like this?" Nadya inquired.

He relaxed immediately. "I am thinking bad thoughts," he said lightly.

"Tell them to me at once," she demanded.

"I had rather forget them," he replied, and she did not ask again.

They sped across the countryside, and oh, the magnificent roads, he thought, and what would not Napoleon have given for them when he had dared to attack Russia? Or Hitler in his turn, for that matter? Yet perhaps the Russians were wise not to build roads across their wilderness, for conquerors, too, come marching along such roads. But did roads matter now when all the skies were open?

"There is your jaw set hard again," Nadya declared, examining him.

He laughed. "Bad habit! I ought to chew gum."

Nadya was immediately excited. "Malcolm, you will not chew the gum! Everything I can like but not this chewing——"

She chewed exaggeratedly, and Lise screamed laughter. "Oh, Mamá, you look so ugly!"

Nadya flashed her eyes at her child. "So will you also if you chew the gum."

"Well, well, we won't chew gum," Malcolm said.

Peter lifted up his voice. "But if every American is chewing the gum, Mamá, will it not seem we are not American if we do not also?"

"We shall be otherwise very American," Nadya said with decision, "but not this."

"Yet if a boy says to me——"

"Tell him you have a very queer mamá, she does not like the chewing of the gum. I take the blame, Peter." She beat her breast softly. "It is I, my son, I who will make you miserable!"

They laughed at her fondly as they delighted to do, and Malcolm blessed the day that had brought him Nadya, she who lightened all darkness, a wellspring of love and gaiety. What was more precious in a man's house than gaiety? He had grown up without it. His mother had been a faithful wife, a firmly affectionate mother, a good housekeeper, but the steady good sense in her eyes never flickered and danced. She was a gray woman and she dimmed the sunshine, never knowing that she did. His father had a dry, bitter humor, mirthless while it amused. Corinne was like their mother; and Susanna, the younger sister, he had known only as a round-faced child, a slip of a girl with secrets in her eyes. He had not imagined gaiety until he went to China and found it in the Chinese. That was the year of the great famine, too, the first one he had ever seen, and the streets were swarming with ragged, half-starving people, begging their way southward. He had been shocked then by the quips they threw at each other, words he could not understand, but which must have been funny for they roused laughter until more in mirth than pity, the bowls of the beggars were filled with copper coins.

"Are they really laughing?" he had asked his young Chinese interpreter.

"They are saying very funny things about you, sir,

while they are starving," the interpreter had replied, smiling in spite of himself.

He had himself surmised that some of the laughter was at him, a tall, grave young American, but he was too shy to ask further. Later, when he learned Chinese in his thoroughgoing fashion, he understood very well and then did not care, for the laughter held no malice. And all this had prepared him for Nadya; it had taught him to comprehend at once the precious quality in her gaiety, a true gaiety, based upon a natural and invincible happiness, an uncontrollable joy.

"Nadya!" he said suddenly.

They were driving now on the smooth roads between the blue hills of Virginia. Redbud and dogwood were coming into bloom and the gardens of old houses were bright with yellow daffodils in thick and ancient clumps. The air was mild and the children had opened the windows.

"A question, Malcolm?" Nadya inquired when he hesitated.

"No, something to say," he replied. "I have often felt it, but never spoken it to you, and this is selfish of me. I will tell you now."

He had taught himself to tell her when he praised her in his heart. That he had resolved to do for his wife. Once as a boy he had come upon his mother in the kitchen, crying soundlessly while she washed the dishes. He was fifteen years old but he had been terrified.

"Mother, what is the matter? Are you sick?" he had asked.

She had stopped her tears at once, and after a moment she had said. "When you get married, Malcolm, tell your wife once in a while if she does something nice."

"Is that all, Mother?" he had inquired when she said no more.

"You just remember that," she had replied.

At the time he had thought it very little, but looking back with the understanding of maturity, he knew now that she often did what she called "nice" things for his father, and that his father, the dark Scot, for the MacNeils were all black Scots, did not feel it right to give praise. Criticism, his father said, it was a man's duty to give, but he expected of his family only what was good and why speak of the good? Therefore, his mother's tears had taught him, in spite of his natural shyness, to tell Nadya not only his love but his praise.

"What do you tell me?" Nadya inquired. She knew him well and the slight flush rising up his neck informed her that somethng delightful was coming from him to her.

"I am grateful to you, my love, for being a gay sort of woman. I enjoy laughter and I can't make it myself."

She understood at once and her vivid face grew tender. "I like so much to laugh."

"It is not only that you laugh," he said, remembering. "But you could laugh even when your family lived in that miserable *hutung* in Peking and you went every day to teach in the university in order to keep from starving. I went miles out of my way to meet you, just so that I could see your bright face."

She put her cheek against his arm. "It is easy to be gay now. There are only gay good things in my life. Yes, I was always gay, it is my nature so, but perhaps because I had nothing and so I made my gaiety out of nothing. Now I have everything—even a country again, Malcolm. for your country is mine. You have given it to me, your wife."

Her feelings and thoughts came from her easily in words. She spoke many languages, English less well than any, but her melodious and fluent Chinese was the purest Peking Mandarin, her French was crisp and swift, and he had heard her speak German with a guttural almost native. Russian he did not understand, but when she was wounded, when inadvertently he had hurt her, although he had learned his lessons in that and it was not often he who hurt her now, but others, or life itself, some suffering not her own which her natural pity compelled her to share could hurt her, and then she sobbed in Russian—a strange language, he thought, sounding like no other he knew, a language that had its roots in deep northern music. She was articulate, but then, so was he, and yet he could not speak as she did, thoughtlessly, it seemed, certainly without effort, and yet every word conveying an exactitude so spontaneous that it amounted to an art. He was articulate enough within himself, or when it came to the silent process of writing, but speech was her medium.

"I hope this will never seem a foreign country to you," he said. "Certainly it is different enough from Manchuria or North China."

"Yet not from Russia," she said, so quickly that it might have been merely a continuation of what he was saying. She waved her hand toward the landscape. "This is so much like Russia, which I cannot really remember, but only imagine I do remember, the red earth, the thin white birches, the evergreen pines, and here and there a flowering tree, but not these flowering trees, that I know, except that in Siberia there is a dogwood. I have heard of it, but how like to this it may be I do not know."

Her lively interest was engaged, and she gazed from the open window. "This much I know is like Russia, Malcolm, for there, as here, is land where nobody is living."

He had no wish to send her thoughts back to that forbidden country and he remarked that it must be time for lunch and that within an hour or so they would be at the house.

The mansion stood on a knoll at the foot of a wooded mountain, a peak in a range of mountains. It was set back far from the road, and the road itself was little traveled. It was still a dirt road, five miles and more off the hard black highway along which they had traveled all day. Fences, no longer white, stretched on either side of a stone-pillared gate, and among a few old trees in the distance Malcolm saw the double portico of his ancestral home. His years in China had deepened his family feeling, and the word ancestral rolled upon his tongue. They left the car at the gate and walked up a wide gravelly path.

"Imagine great oaks along this road," he said. "I can just remember them when I was about your age, Peter."

They were silent a moment, conscious instinctively of the presence of a history they had not shared.

"How much pity those trees were cut down!" Nadya exclaimed.

"There are still two by the house," Lise said.

The house was inhabited, for the windows upstairs were open and thin white curtains fluttered out. Downstairs the huge front door was open and half a dozen spotted hunting dogs slept on the porch between the columns. They opened their eyes and growled but did not bark. Malcolm lifted the heavy brass knocker and let it fall, but no one came, and they stood looking through the big bare hall which went straight through the house and opened again on the lawns at the back.

"I remember this hall full of fine French furniture," he told them. "My grandmother was French and she liked French things."

"Ah, French furniture is always beautiful," Nadya sighed.

Her lively glance searched the space before her. "But the staircase is so beautiful also!" she exclaimed. "What is that dark wood, Malcolm?"

"Black walnut," he said, although he had not remembered it for years, "and the oak leaves on the panels are hand-carved. Some uncle or other of my grandfather's carved wood for a hobby and the panels were his contribution. I remember that there are closets in the dining room which he carved, too, with the old crest of my father's family, two willow trees over a spring."

A door opened and a tall, thin man, lean-faced, with a small white moustache and goatee, came toward them. He wore a gray shirt and mud-stained trousers tucked into high leather boots.

"Strangers, come in," he drawled. "What can I do for you?"

Malcolm put out his hand. "This was once my great-grandfather's house, and I wanted my children to see it. This is my wife, my son, my daughter."

"Come in—come in," the man said. "I'm Captain Boulter. I reckon you knew my father bought the place from your great-uncle. I live here myself now all alone, a widow man. I gave up my own place, higher on the mountain, after my son Phil said he didn't want to live here. Till then we lived here in the winter and up in my own place in the summer. It's handier near the road. Come in—this is the parlor, or was, in your family's time, I reckon. I use it for my office. I farm two thousand acres of this valley land, all fine loam. You can pick it up anywhere and it's soft as silk in your hand—not a stone in it. I raise cattle and hogs."

They followed him as he talked and gazed into the half-empty rooms. Fine paneling and polished hardwood floors were all that remained of the past. The windows were curtainless except for the shoddy white cotton curtains in the rooms upstairs. The beds were iron, mattresses bare, and the dining room was the owner's bedroom. There a wide iron bed lay tumbled and the wooden chairs were half covered with rough clothing.

"A widow man has to make out the best he can," the Captain said cheerfully. "My beloved wife was sick for a long, long time, and my two boys went off to the wars and one never came back. The other one don't get along with me, or his wife don't—it's the same thing. I never had any daughters, and while my beloved wife lay dying, I had to manage with field women as house help. Niggers aren't what they were, either. They come and they go. These here great big old places, Mr. MacNeil, were designed different. They were planned for niggers to stay on the place. If I can get my land plowed and the seed sowed ever' spring, I have to be content. A nigger girl, Morene, cooks my meals and cleans when she feels like it. I don't harvest my corn. I turn the hogs into it and let 'em take care of themselves. My cattle I sell on the hoof."

And while he talked he led them through the house. The staunch and beautiful mansion remained as it had been built, silent under desecration, and Malcolm yearned over it. He longed to restore it to what it had been when his great-grandfather built it, to replant the avenue of trees and cut away the rotting vines on the portico. He might even collect the furniture that belonged here. Finding it and setting it into place again would be a delightful task. And could there be a better way to plant roots for his children in a country they must make their own?

He did not speak until they finished their tour and had seen even the fields, now being plowed. A score of black and filthy men were working on the land and their master bellowed at their foreman.

"Sam, don't you let that lazy lot of loafers think they

can quit before they finish the west acreage! Sundown won't make any difference to me or them if it ain't finished."

"Nossuh," Sam mumbled. He was a huge, loose-jointed man, stoop-shouldered and sullen-faced. He stared at Nadya and the children, and she looked back at him directly, a strange shadow in her too expressive eyes. Then she turned abruptly away.

Captain Boulter saw both look and movement. He gave a guffaw. "Sam, you ain't very pretty," he drawled. "You better get back on the job."

The hulking man bowed his head and tramped his way across the field.

Malcolm felt he must explain. "My wife has not lived in America before and she is not accustomed to dark skins."

Nadya rejected his explanation sharply. "It is not the dark skin, Malcolm, not at all! I care nothing how are skins, you know that!"

He comprehended a mood in her which he did not wish to reveal to a stranger.

"Ah, well," he said, "we must get on our way."

But when they were ready to get in the car again his nostalgia was not to be restrained and he turned to the Captain and asked, half-carelessly, "I don't suppose you want to sell the old place back to me?"

Caution crept into the shrewd small blue eyes staring at him. "Well, I might at that. I've been thinkin' of retirin'. I'm past sixty-five, though I don't look it, folks tell me. What would you consider payin'?"

Before Malcolm could answer, Nadya, already seated in the car, leaned toward him from the open door. "Malcolm, if you please, no, my dear! I could not live here. The mountains, the loneliness——" She waved her hands toward the lofty peaks above the house.

Malcolm nodded. "Sorry, Captain! I should have discussed it with my wife first."

"That's all right," Captain Boulter answered, always amiable. "I know how womenfolk are. I learned early to ask my beloved wife first. It always paid." He gave his great guffaw again, leaned lazily on the gate, and waved them down the muddy road.

"You must forgive me, please, Malcolm," Nadya said breathlessly. "I am sure it would be not a good place for us. For me, impossible! It was not that the man was black, Malcolm, not at all. I admire sometimes a shining black skin. No, it was his eyes. Malcolm, such were the eyes of my father's serfs in Russia!"

He was strangely nettled for once by her emotion. "You never saw them, Nadya."

"Ah, no, but my mother did tell me how she felt when she looked at the serfs and so I felt when I looked at that black man. And not only in Russia, Malcolm, but also in China. I saw such eyes there, too, in the fields, in the valleys between the mountains outside the walls of Peking."

"But what eyes, Nadya?" He spoke carefully that he might not show impatience.

"Savage and wonder," she said in a suddenly solemn voice, "ignorant and angry. It is dangerous. I cannot stay where are such people. Malcolm, let us go far away. You did not tell me there are such people here, too."

These were the old memories, he told himself, memories she had inherited from her parents, memories that she had made for herself in her childhood in Manchuria, a thin, fair child fighting her way among the Chinese street children of Harbin.

"I am afraid there are such people in every country," he said, "but we will go as far away from them as we can."

They traveled northward in unusual quiet. He spoke of casual things and decided suddenly, in midafternoon, to turn aside and take them sightseeing to Monticello. They must meet Thomas Jefferson on his own ground and make friends with his ghost. So let them learn new memories!

The afternoon was mild, and the windless sunlight fell through trees whose branches were still delicately leafed. Build upon a mountain, Thomas Jefferson had declared, never in the valley, and let the mansion be set in a natural park, a forest grown by the accident of seed fall and bird flight, clearing only enough for the vistas of distance.

Malcolm, driving slowly up the wide road to the mansion, discoursed amiably to his family about Thomas Jefferson. "He was a tall fellow, red-haired and slender. He had blue-gray eyes, very clear, and a straight nose and a full underlip. He loved his country as he loved his home, and the two loves are the same. He planned that house you see up there until it was exactly suited to him and therefore it is like no other house on earth. Even when it was finished he changed the whole inside of it. He tore out the central stairs and made narrow private stairs. He loved privacy. He liked to call himself a farmer, but he was everything besides. He was a scientist and a musician, he understood history, he was fond of gadgets—you'll see how his bed was lowered at night and drawn up again to the ceiling in the morning, and right above his bed is a little room where his manservant slept. The whole place is the living portrait of a man who believed in being himself. The glorious and unique thing about him was that he wanted everyone else to feel the same way."

They reached the house, and they descended. Other tourists were before them; his children were still shy of Americans, and immediately Lise clung to his hand.

Even Nadya, he observed, looked at the strangers curiously, as though she did not belong to their kind. Well, this was his task, to be done slowly and thoroughly, until they recognized in any American something of themselves.

"But this house is not beautiful, Malcolm," Nadya said with surprise. The air at this height lifted the tendrils of her blond hair and waved them gently about her face, and her blue eyes were lively. She paused to gaze at the domed building, her red lower lip pinched reflectively between thumb and forefinger. "A very independent house, yes," she decided, "not common! Let us go into it."

Her practical eye assessed each room as they strolled through the mansion. She was asking herself, as Malcolm could see, how she would like to live in such a house, its mistress and manager. In the Peking house she had been efficient and charming, a woman able to rouse devotion in her servants. But Chinese servants are the very aristocracy of all servants, self-respecting, proud, loving those whom they serve, if these are worthy of love. What enemies they could be when they did not love, he had seen in other houses than his.

They wandered slowly, observing every detail, and then they discovered the rooms for the slaves under the terraces. The sight gravely shook Nadya's nascent admiration for the builder of so independent a house.

"Lise, look, and Peter, you see—" she exclaimed. "This is not good, these dark small rooms for the black people, damp too, doubtless, although on the hill. Malcolm, this is not right. It was like this in Russia, too, and it was not good."

Tourists stared at her with eyes suddenly hostile.

"So we found, my dear," Malcolm replied quietly. "The rooms are empty now. There was a war about it."

Oh, how he had to teach these three before they

were sound Americans! Perhaps he had begun wrongly with the past. Better, perhaps, to march boldly here and now upon some American town, buy a house, and begin to live in it. Learning and living were always inseparable, just as in China he had never learned even the language until he gave up the comfortable bachelor quarters of the young diplomats and rented two rooms with a Chinese family. Professor Ren had taught him articulately enough but Mrs. Ren had taught him wordlessly as she superintended her complex household of elderly parents, a widowed aunt, two orphaned cousins, and such relatives as belong in any ancestral home. In the midst of the generations the three Ren children grew up healthy and happy, depending upon one adult or another, as the moment favored. Thus when Professor Ren slapped his children sharply, driven beyond patience because he needed quiet for his work, the old grandfather would totter out and shield the young ones with his delicate old hands, saying nothing, but mutely signifying that a child must not be at the mercy of an angry adult. In old China, to be angry, Malcolm had learned, was to be temporarily demented. The children fled shrieking to the old man and he had gathered them into his robes and led them away. After quiet had prevailed for an hour or so, the grandmother prepared tea and sent the children to take it to the father. Propitiation and harmony, these two words the aged grandfather brushed carefully upon a large sheet of white paper, and he had taught the children that day to sing them over and over. Then with a little flour and water, stirred to a paste, with his forefinger, he had put the paper on the wall at the level of the children's eyes.

In such small ways Malcolm had learned how to live in China until he had made that country his own, and its people his people. Now he must reverse the process for his wife and children. Here where he had been born and reared, they must learn and live, and the process would be the same, except that there were no gentle grandparents. There were, however, his two sisters, Corinne and Susanna.

"Well," he said, "it is time that we moved on."

That night, following his thesis that they must begin to live wherever they were, he stopped at a clean string of rooms along the highway.

"Here is where we spend the night," he announced.

"An hotel, Malcolm?" Nadya asked.

"A motel," he replied, "and there is a difference."

It was a comfortable place, close to the earth, and between the adjoining rooms there was a shower bath where the water spouted with such energy that Lise cried out, "Needles, Papá!" His children called him Papá, the last syllable accented in Nadya's fashion, or they called him Babushka.

Nadya looked about her with wonder. She examined the cotton sheets, the cotton blankets. "Is it for the poor, then, Malcolm?" she inquired.

"It is for anybody," he said, "anybody at all."

"It is quite clean," she replied.

What she was thinking he did not know. She undressed thoughtfully and went into the shower and came back again, and standing in her long white silk nightgown, she brushed the drops of water out of her golden hair. A beautiful woman, he thought, though regretting her long hair again as his eyes dwelled upon her, and he pitied all men whose wives were not beautiful. Love, he granted, did not depend upon beauty, but a man can thank God if there is also beauty.

He stood, seeing her lovely body outlined through the sheer material, seeing her face smiling at him in the mirror while she went on brushing her hair. He was too experienced a lover, too adept, to approach her quickly. Foreplay for them began not in the physical. It began, as it was now beginning, in the smile exchanged, the lingering look, the small signs of her readiness, her lack of haste as she continued to brush her hair, turning her head this way and that, catching his steady gaze in the mirror and turning away to catch it again and yet again —all signs he knew and recognized. She was not a blatant lover. There was an Asian delicacy in her invitation which stirred him as no bold advance could ever have done.

He moved to close the door between the two rooms and came back to her, still not touching her. She put down her silver-backed brush.

"I think already the children are sleeping," she said.

It was her way of beginning.

"But will you not find this room too strange?" he asked.

It was his way of response, considerate though eager.

"You are here, I am here," she said softly.

She turned to him, her eyes upon his. She put out her arms to him and he enfolded her, while she talked.

"So how is it strange, anywhere in the world, if we are alone together? See, I am so shameless! I drew all the curtains closed. I pinned big safety pin with them, even—while you are with the children. How bold, is it not? I am learning. All these years it takes me to learn —when it is the time for us both."

He silenced her with his lips on hers, his hand slipping the silken straps of her nightgown until the garment fell at her feet. Then he carried her, naked, and laid her on the bed.

"Why do you think I chose this room with one big bed?" he asked, half laughing. "Now lie there, my *ai-ren*, until I make myself clean. And mind you think of nothing but me, until I come back to you—a few minutes—I promise you!"

He went into the bathroom then and showered, lathering himself with the special soap he had carried with him ever since he found that she liked its Chinese scent. *Ai-ren*—the new words that the young Chinese were using—"loved one," husband, wife, lover—all were the same with him and Nadya.

She was fastidious, nevertheless, this *ai-ren*, this loved one of his, and she had taught him in her delicate but honest fashion how to win her love, too, the physical ways, first the immaculate cleanliness, even his hair, then a special scent, then a slow approach, no words, except a murmured few, gentleness in the beginning—oh, great gentleness and no demand—while——

But now he was ready, and he returned to the room. She lay upon the bed, naked as he had left her, her slender hands clasped across her breasts. He stretched himself beside her and slowly unclasping her hands, he kissed her breasts, one and the other, long, lingering kisses. She sighed, she smiled, she met his eyes gazing into hers.

"And does it matter," she inquired, half-playfully, "does it matter at all what country we make love, what house, what room, what hour, day and night, so long as we are alone together?"

She drew down his head before he spoke, and he answered with his lips on hers.

Sometime in the night, he did not know the hour, he was waked from deep sleep. A bony young hand groped over his face. He seized it and knew it was Peter's hand. He felt his son's sweet breath on his cheek in a whisper of sound.

"Babushka, shall you not come into my bed? I am not sleeping."

Peter had been a child frightened of the night, but that had been long ago. It had been years since this had happened, and Peter was no longer a child.

"I will come," he whispered, astonished, and with Peter's hand in his, they went into the other room. Lise was sleeping. He got into bed with Peter, moving as far as he could but the bed was so narrow that Peter, lying down, clung to him to keep from falling out. Malcolm put an arm around his shoulder.

"Now," he whispered, "what is this?"

"Babushka," Peter said in the faintest whisper of reply, "I like America—it is not that."

"No?"

"No," Peter said. "Not at all. Truly I respect America very much. Such a large big house today on the hill! But please——"

"Yes, Peter?"

"Let us go back home, please! Please, sir, dear Babushka, take us again to Peking! There I like it best of all."

He held the boy's trembling body close and very well he understood that yearning for the life that had been.

"We must not wake Lise," he said in his son's ear. Indeed, Nadya, too, must not hear this.

"I don't wake her, Papá," Peter said. "I come only to you. Please, let us go home again where we were!"

How could he tell the boy? That home which they had loved did not now exist. The life that had been was no more. A fierce new wind blew down from the north over the mighty old city and the past was gone. Whatever was to be, it was never what they had known. But how to tell a trembling boy such bitter truth?

"Peter, can you hear me when I whisper like this?"

"I hear you, Papá."

"We cannot go back, Peter."

"Why, Papá?"

"Because what you remember is no longer there."

"Our house is there, Papá, and Peking is there."

"Ah, but it was the people who made it a happy place for you! Now the people no longer love us, they do not want us there."

"But why, Papá? We are not changed."

"I cannot explain to you why they no longer love us, Peter. Our old friends do, of course, Wang Ma and Professor Ren and Mrs. Ren, and such people do love us but it is dangerous for them to love us and so it is better that we went away and came to our own country. After all, China was not our country, Peter."

"I liked it."

"So did I, very much. And we will like our own country, too. You wait and see. I promise you."

He felt Peter shiver once or twice but he said no more, and at last the boy slept. It had been well to say simply what was true. There could be no return. The past was no more, and the only road lay straight ahead.

He remembered his sister Corinne as a thin, dark, intense girl, secretly consumed with anxiety lest no presentable man would invite her to marriage. Thin, dark, and intense, she had insisted upon going to college, to prepare herself, she said, for a career. Every girl ought to have a career, she said, but what she had meant was that every girl ought to have an excuse for living if she could not marry. They had all been relieved when Charles Barkman, the junior vice-president of the local bank, had proposed to her. Whether she had been in love was questionable, Malcolm knew. She had not behaved like a girl in love and she did not look now like a woman who had ever been in love. But then, he was spoiled with love, for he had Nadya.

"Well, Corinne," he said upon the afternoon of their arrival, "we are on your doorstep, Peter and Lise, Nadya and I. We are a little late because we could not refrain from going around by Monticello."

Corinne was briskly cheerful. "Come in, come in," she said in brisk staccato. "Charles had to go back to the office, and the children are at school, but I'm here. Have you had lunch?"

She addressed herself to Malcolm, agitated, as he could see, by the arrival of strange relatives.

"I know better than to arrive with four for lunch," he said.

"As if!" Corinne retorted. She ushered them into a large neat living room. "Sit down and let me look at you," she exclaimed. She was slender, erect, and well-dressed, and her brown hair, slightly tinted, was evenly waved. She was the sort of woman, Malcolm saw, who looked so young that she must be forty-five. Forty-five, he calculated, was her exact age. They seated themselves.

"Or would you rather go to your rooms right away?" Corinne exclaimed.

She was as fidgety as ever, he noticed, under that bright, brisk surface. She would be hard on the children, maybe, and Nadya frankly did not know what to make of her. Upon Nadya's beautiful face there was a look of wonder.

"You do not at all look like Malcolm." This was Nadya's look, too soon followed by the words.

Corinne laughed, the same quick, mirthless laugh that he remembered. "No, Malcolm was always tall," she replied.

She examined her sister-in-law swiftly and sharply. A pretty woman, she thought, in a foreign sort of way. Yet whatever had Malcolm been thinking of, to marry a Russian! And the children as foreign as the mother! What a complication!

"I'm sure you are tired," she said, kindly, neverthe-

less. "We can talk later. You children must make yourselves at home. There's a rumpus room downstairs
where you can play, or you can go outdoors."

She rose, and they followed her as she led the way
up the carpeted stairs. She threw open two doors.

"I've given you these two rooms, you can take your
choice, only I advise the larger one for the grown-ups.
The smaller one is next to the back stairs, and the children will find it convenient to slip down that way when
they want to go outside. The bathroom is between."

"I haven't seen this house," Malcolm said. "Do you
like New York better than Virginia?"

"Oh, much," Corinne was eager to affirm how much.
"The atmosphere here is so pleasant, so friendly. There
is something exciting about a city, you know, Malcolm.
I never felt Mother and Dad really liked that little
southern town, did you?"

"I never thought about it," Malcolm said honestly.

"Oh, they didn't," Corinne insisted. "And Charles
likes it ever so much better here, too. The people are
conservative, of course. Maybe that's why we like it so
much."

It was empty talk, the noises that people make when
they must get acquainted and do not know how to
begin the process. "We'll wash and be down," he said
abruptly. "Meanwhile the bags—I'd forgotten!"

Corinne laughed again. "I'm sorry we don't have
servants of the sort you are used to. I suppose over
there you had a houseful of them."

"No more," he replied. "Come along, Peter. You're in
America and you carry your own bags."

He seized his son's hand, and they ran downstairs to
the car.

"Such a nice room," Nadya said. She stood in the
center of the green and white room, appreciating its
cleanliness and order. With deep instinct she divined

that this sister of Malcolm's was a foreigner who must be charmed, and therefore she must be charming. She had known so many people, of so many kinds, and few like herself, to whom she could speak directly and at once, as now she would like to have spoken to this one. She would like to have put her arms around Corinne and said to her, "I love you because you are the sister of my beloved." But this would be to frighten the thin, correct woman still more. Yes, Corinne was wary and so she must coax her gently to love.

"A home," Nadya said. She sank into the comfortable chair by the brick fireplace. "Oh, wonderful to be in a home! You make it so pleasant here. Your children and your husband must be very happy."

Corinne smiled. "I try to make them happy. Of course it takes work. Charles works hard and so do I. It takes a lot to support a family now. And of course we want the best for our two sons."

"Of course," Nadya agreed warmly. "And I think they have the best."

Corinne considered a reply to this. "Well, please make yourself comfortable," she said finally. "Come downstairs when you're ready."

She smiled politely and tripped away, high heels clacking delicately on the polished floors between the rugs.

Malcolm and Peter returned with the bags, and the children busied themselves with unpacking. Malcolm threw himself in the chair opposite Nadya. The brick fireplace was between them, small logs laid neatly for a fire, the hearth swept clean of ashes.

"Well, my love?" Malcolm inquired. His wife's vivid face still expressed bewilderment, her vague smile confusion, doubt, a mild anxiety.

"I like your sister," Nadya said resolutely. "When she allows me, I will love her."

"Does she forbid?" Malcolm inquired.

"I think she is not used to love," Nadya replied.

At the door Peter appeared suddenly, a pile of disordered garments hanging from his hands.

"Mamá," he said, "when do we go away from here?"

"Oh, naughty," Nadya murmured. She rose and went to him and put her arms around him. "Wicked one," she went on. "We have only just come! We will stay some days, and you must like everything. These are your flesh and blood, your aunt, the sister of Papá, and her husband, your uncle, and the children, your cousins. It is important to have a family, Peter. It is necessary to help them to love you. Think how fortunate you are, how much more fortunate than was I, whose uncles and aunts were entirely liquidated! We can never thank Papá enough that he could bring us all to America. Dear ones, we have a family, a true family, our own!"

Lise was listening, too. Lise she was winning, Lise was beginning to smile. "I will go downstairs and wait for my cousins," she announced.

"I shall stay here and read," Peter said.

Nadya drew down her mouth at him and picked up the garments that were dropping to the floor. "No, Peter! Not reading yet!" Reading was Peter's retreat from the unstable world.

"Let him do what he likes," Malcolm said abruptly. "His cousins will see that he goes outdoors. I imagine they're an active pair. Most American boys are."

"You are too kind, Malcolm," Nadya said and she went to him and kissed him.

It was a casual kiss, lightly bestowed but with warmth, and he caught her about the waist and held her for an instant. "Thank God, you're soft to hold. I adore soft women!"

She laughed richly, "Please, Malcolm," she said, "adore only me!"

The children watched them and smiled in unconscious sympathy. These two adults belonging to them were always in love. It was silly and funny and it made their noses tickle, but they liked it. They were diverted and reassured.

"Peter, do please come downstairs with me!" Lise exclaimed.

"Oh, all right, I will," Peter said, forgetting retreat.

Malcolm watched his sister with a large thoughtfulness as she tripped neatly about the kitchen. It was evening and she was preparing the dinner, with which he felt it impossible to aid her. Nadya's help she had refused, saying in her curt, not unkind fashion, "No, I prefer not to have help before dinner. Afterwards anybody can help. I hate washing dishes."

"You ought to have a servant, Corinne," he said now.

"Nobody has servants any more," she answered, "not since the war. The most worthless colored maid nowadays would rather work in a noisy, dusty factory than in a clean, quiet kitchen. They are all too good for it."

A bitter edge in her voice make him understand that she too hated her clean quiet kitchen but food must be prepared and there was only herself to do it. He wondered with some surprise why he was so much more perceptive than he used to be. Perhaps because he was older, but perhaps, too, it was because he had spent years among the Chinese, a humanistic people, sensitive to every atmosphere of feeling and living so close to one another that peace was essential. And peace could only be the fruit of a profound human understanding, a continuing delicacy of perceptive feeling.

Corinne stood by the stove, making, as he could see, superlative french fried potatoes. She wore a ruffled white apron and not a wave of her hair was disturbed. In her way she was now a handsome woman, though taut in every nerve, and even the carefully smoothed lines of her face did not hide the tensity beneath. Now why, he speculated, should she look as though she controlled only by the utmost exertion of her will some intolerable mood or circumstance of her life? Something was wrong here, the very perfection of the house was meaningful.

"Dear," he said with real yearning over this sister of his, "can't I do something to help you?"

She flashed a quick look at him and relented slightly. "Since you're not company, you may get the ice cubes from the refrigerator and put them in that silver pitcher. Fill it from the faucet—not that one, but the one over the hand basin. Our water is hard and we have a softener, but we like to drink the hard water."

He strolled across the kitchen to do her bidding. "A water softener? I hadn't heard of that luxury."

Above the hiss of the hot fat she lifted her voice. "We must have some compensations, yet all the machines can't take the place of one really competent person. I suppose you had five or six servants in China?"

"That is all past," he reminded her. "You can't imagine the change, since the Communists took over. Nadya says her father said it was the same in Russia when the revolution broke. What was on top went under and what was under came up. Her family, of course, went under and barely escaped with their lives. That is why I got out of China early. I didn't want her to go through that again, nor the children."

She lifted her head to listen but not to him. Voices were in the hall.

"That's Charles and the boys!"

The door opened immediately and a tall man with a small, firm paunch came in, his hand outstretched.

"Hello!" he said, accenting the last syllable. "Well, Malcolm, this is a surprise, in a way. We weren't sure just when you'd arrive. Glad to see you—it's been a long time. I saw the kids outside—a nice-looking pair."

He shook hands and went to kiss his wife's cheek. "How have you been, hon?"

"Oh, nothing unusual," Corinne said, without looking up.

"Guess I'll wash up," Charles said.

"Dinner will be ready in fifteen minutes," Corinne said. "Tell the boys to come in, will you?"

A moment later his nephews stood at the door, grinning and shy, rather handsome, Malcolm was pleased to see, especially the elder one, a slender dark-haired fellow, as different as possible from the tubby younger boy.

"Where were you?" Corinne asked sharply.

"Talking to Nadya—she doesn't want us to call her Aunt—" the tubby boy said.

"Speak to your uncle," Corinne directed. "Malcolm, this is Charles junior, and Robert."

"Otherwise Charley and Bob," the young Charles said. He had a fine smile and he put out his hand to his uncle. "Glad to see you, sir."

"Hello," Bob said in a colorless voice, coming no nearer.

"Go and wash up, boys," Corinne said. "Dinner in ten minutes."

"I had better go and collect my own young," Malcolm said.

He was inexplicably glad to leave the kitchen atmosphere. It was a bright and well-furnished place but the air was not cheerful, for Corinne was not cheerful, and the three male creatures under her command were subdued to her mood, as he already saw. There had been some of this in his own childhood, and enough of it so that he now recalled that when he came from school he was sometimes delighted to linger in the kitchen near his mother, and yet at other times he was repelled without knowing why, exiled by darkness in her look and her silence. He returned to the living room to see the light of the electric floor lamp shining down upon Nadya's lovely head. She was absorbed in a magazine, a brightly colored affair, portraying fantastic foods and love scenes sandwiched together, as he could see over her shoulder. She looked up at him and pointed at a full-page salad.

"Do not expect these dishes from me, please, Malcolm! I shall be unable."

"Thank God," he said fervently and bent to kiss her warm lips.

On the third evening of their visit Nadya, who had grown increasingly thoughtful and gentle as the days passed, stood at the dressing table brushing her fair hair. They were ready to leave early in the morning, their bags were packed, and upon the excuse of this they had come early to bed.

"I tell you something, Malcolm," Nadya said in a dreamy voice.

"What is it?" he asked.

"Your sister is very unhappy." Pathos and pity deepened her voice. She looked at him in the mirror.

"Now what makes you think that?" he asked.

"She is not in love with her husband," Nadya said in the voice of tragedy.

Malcolm was skeptical and rational. "They have been married a good many years, Nadya."

She turned on him in a whirl of short, flying hair. "Malcolm, you should be ashamed! Please, you know what I mean. If I am like that to you, I will ask you to kill me——"

He laughed. "Which I would never do—" and he kissed her fervently.

"Now you do know what I mean?" she demanded.

He tangled his hands in her hair and pulled back her head and kissed her again. "I know that there is only one you," he said. "I doubt there is another like you, even in Russia—not any more! The Communists have women like machines now, I daresay. I have the only living example of a real woman."

Nadya shook with soft laughter, burying her face in his shoulder. "I must also say that Charles, the husband of Corinne, is not like you, Malcolm! Such a fat little belly, isn't it? What does he keep there, Malcolm? The other parts of him are so thin."

"Shame on you," he said.

She smoothed his bare belly with admiration. "Malcolm, you are nicely hollow, yet you did eat dinner very well. For this I myself envy you. Hollow I am not, but also not otherwise. Shall we have soon another baby, Malcolm, born in America?"

He pushed her away, pretending fright. "Now, Nadya, you know I have already said no to your propositions! We must get settled, my love, we must make a home. I must decide what I want to do, a job or not a job. The children must go to school properly. The new home first, my love, and then we'll see whether we want to add to its population."

He saw mischief in her teasing eyes and knew her quite capable of carrying such mischief into the most willful and flagrant conduct. That was the unending charm of her. Few husbands, he secretly believed, had the pleasure of resisting the enticement of a wife. To resist successfully now gave him a feeling of strength and superiority, added to which was the exciting knowledge that he could always yield without disaster. Nevertheless, tonight he did not yield. He was really quite serious about not having more children—not yet. Beyond that, however, was a curious reserve. He did not want to make love here in his sister's house. Nadya's intuition was uncanny. For only this afternoon he had been alone with Corinne, Charley and Bob having taken Nadya and the children to a baseball game, their first and therefore important. He had not gone with them, because Corinne had not wanted to go, and she had signified in small ways that she had something to tell him.

"I feel you should be prepared for Susanna," she had said when the house was quiet. They were sitting on the pleasant front porch. The day was unseasonably warm and white tulips were blooming in the flower beds.

"Is something wrong with Susanna?" he inquired.

Corinne lit a cigarette. Her hands, he thought, were pitiful, thin and corrugated with veins, though fastidiously cared for. Even her nails were long and painted brightly pink. When she washed dishes she drew on rubber gloves. But she smoked without grace or ease, quickly and nervously, puffing her carefully rouged lips and pressing off the ash too soon into the ashtray on a small wrought iron table.

"I hate to have to tell you about Susanna," she said in her sharp fashion.

"Must I be told?" he inquired.

"I am afraid someone else will tell you—or that she will tell you herself."

"Why not let her tell me herself?"

"She won't tell you the truth, that's why!" She threw him a sharp look from her sad gray eyes. "She looks on the whole affair as a romance—a romance at her age, mind you!"

"It's an affair, is it?"

"I don't know what else to call it, and everybody knows about it except Hartley, her own husband!"

"How do you know about it, Corinne?"

"She told me," Corinne said. She rubbed her nose in irritation. "I wish she hadn't. But she can't help talking —you'll see! And she'll want your advice, but I warn you she will have no idea of taking it. She asks for advice so that she can talk about her lover."

"It's gone as far as that, has it?"

"Of course it has. A woman always knows." She waited for his reply and when he kept silent, she hurried on. "I don't understand Susanna at all. Where is her conscience? That's what I said to her. 'Susanna, where is your conscience?' It's not as if Hartley were the sort to do the same thing. He isn't—he's steady, like Charles, except he doesn't look like Charles. As a matter of fact, he is quite handsome, I must admit. And certainly Susanna was madly in love with him when they were married. She was positively insane about him—so she hasn't *that* excuse!"

"What excuse, Corinne?" He asked this mildly, but with a dreadful foreknowledge of what she might say.

She scarcely hesitated. "I mean that if she hadn't been in love with Hartley, I might have understood that she wanted the experience once—you know—before it was too late. I won't condone what she has done, mind you, for if we all did what she has, where would our society be, and what would become of the homes? Plenty of women do, of course, but I have never felt it was right."

Life with Nadya had taught him directness and the beauty of nakedness, in spirit as in flesh. "Do you mean that you didn't love Charles when you married him, Corinne?"

She quivered for one instant and then the walls of her heart broke down. Her carefully smooth face flushed and grew turgid. Two veins on her temples swelled and beat. Even the veins on her hands swelled. He said quietly, "I should not have asked that, though I am your brother. But I should be sorry to think you had missed love."

She tried to laugh. "I haven't a single complaint to make against Charles. He has been a good husband and a steady provider and today that is worth a great deal."

He did not reply to this. The dog belonging to his nephews came up the steps and he scratched its ears.

"Charles is a fine man," he said at last, "and he loves you."

"That," she said bitterly, "is what really hurts me. It's not my fault, but I have never been able to give him what he deserves to have—a wife who loves him."

The air between them quivered with tragic reality. He knew instantly that Corinne had never told anyone what she was now telling him, and that she was tearing her heart to pieces with the words she was speaking at last.

"My dear," he said, "how do you know that you don't love him? Perhaps you do, without realizing just what love is."

She rejected his comfort. "Oh, no," she said distinctly. "I know very well. I was in love once with a man who didn't love me. When I saw he never would love me, never could, because he loved his own wife, I married Charles."

"Oh, Corinne!"

She put up her thin, fashionable hand. "It's over, of course. And I'm no fool—I never was. I knew I had no chance. His wife was pretty and charming, and I have never been either. But I loved him anyway, and would again."

How does one speak to a woman like this, he asked himself, a modern woman, he supposed she must be called, intelligent, intense, literal—realistic, he supposed, was the word, as difficult to comfort as to love? And yet she had loved a man and did still love him, as he could discern, though she had said it was over, and the love was bitter, not sweet, because she knew herself unlovely, and this though she knew, too, that she had the profound tragic ability to love with her whole heart. He wondered what Nadya would have done with an unrequited love and could not imagine that any love of hers could be unrequited.

"Perhaps you are happier, nevertheless, Corinne, for having known what love is, even though——"

"No, I can't agree with that," she said in her crisp fashion. "It was plain unmitigated hell, and it still is, even to remember. When I think how I used to wait for him to pass, just that I might look at him, how I used to sit in church so that I could see him!" She tried to laugh, and a dry cackle of sound came from her grinning lips. "I used to stare at him until he felt it and turned his head, and that was joy enough for the rest of the day. I'd think, 'he knows'—but I doubt he did! Inside that handsome body there probably wasn't such a wonderful brain."

She tried to laugh and this time it sounded bitter indeed. "The system is wrong, Malcolm! There is something wrong here with the way women have to stumble into marriage. Maybe it is all right for men—I don't know. But for women like me, too well-educated, perhaps, or educated in the wrong way—I don't know. We're supposed to be equal to men, but we never can be so long as we have to stand and wait for an invitation to marriage. And the devil of it is we still want marriage."

She did very well now at laughter. It was still bitter but true. "Oh, there are plenty of us, but I can't forgive Susanna! She married the man she wanted."

There was nothing to say and he said little enough. "My dear, I thank you for telling me what you have, not about Susanna but about yourself. And I admire you. You are living a brave life."

"Not quite successfully." She was touched and did not want to show that she was, but she quivered with released emotion and she was fighting tears.

"Very successfully," he insisted.

She wiped her eyes quickly, and then attempting her brisk and casual manner, she said, "I think I'll go upstairs for a little while, Malcolm. I am getting to the age now where I have to take a rest somewhere in the day."

He rose, too. "Nonsense," he said. Moved by unexpected affection, he bent and kissed her and was surprised to find how little effort it was. She was embarrassed but pleased and he felt the pat of her dry palm on his cheek.

After she had gone, he sat for a while, glad to be alone. So there was to be no escape from tragedy, after all! It was not, to be sure, the tragedy of beggars and wars, but he supposed that a broken heart was in its way quite as hard to bear as a starving body or wounded flesh. He felt a slight dejection nevertheless, even a mild resentment, that Corinne should have placed upon him the burden of her secret. After all, he could do nothing! He resolved, after some reflection, to be selfish to the extent of telling Nadya.

So now he told her this last night, and she listened, tears filling her eyes. "I am not weeping for Susanna, I am weeping only for Corinne," she informed him. "I cannot weep for Susanna until I see her and know how unhappy is she. But Corinne is so good. I tell you, Malcolm, Corinne is very good. She works too hard and the house is too clean. She works too hard also to be a good wife and mother, and she is too good there also. One cannot work so hard and be also happy, you understand, Malcolm?"

"I understand because I understand you," he replied. It was true. Nadya, being all woman, made him tolerantly, even tenderly understanding of other women. Her large and lenient nature was his background of reference.

Meanwhile he made up his mind that he would not search for any secrets that Susanna might have. If she wished to confide in him he would allow her to do so without revealing what he knew. If she said nothing, neither would he. What might have been necessary for Corinne to reveal might not be necessity for Susanna.

He perceived as soon as he saw his younger sister that the two households would be completely different. They reached Susanna's house in the middle of an afternoon. The mild weather held and the front door was open although they had come north for two hundred miles. The daffodils here were still in bud, but forsythia had broken into a froth of yellow flowers. There was a great deal of it. Susanna had planted it inside the low red brick stone wall that surrounded her house, and the house, a red brick bungalow, lifted its roof from masses of the soft yellow. Susanna had always liked flowers, he remembered, and as a girl it had been she and not their mother who had kept flowers in the big house. He had telephoned ahead the hour of their arrival and Susanna was at home and waiting. When she saw their car come in the driveway she ran out of the house, a pretty woman in a blue flowered print dress, a woman still slender but with curves, and a mass of bright brown hair, short and curled about her head.

"Ah, yes," Nadya whispered. "She is in love, Malcolm!"

There was no time to answer. Susanna was hugging them, her blue eyes laughing, her red lips laughing, and she was trying to kiss them all, one after the other. She gave Nadya a great squeeze, chattering all the while.

"Malcolm, what a lovely wife, you lucky thing! And Peter, and Lise, darlings—and Malcolm, how can you look so much younger than you are? Hartley was simply sick that he couldn't take the afternoon off and of course the girls are still in school. They wanted to stay at home, and I was perfectly willing, it isn't every day I have a brother coming home from China, but Hartley thought they shouldn't and of course we always obey our daddy."

She was dragging at their bags, insisting that she must help, and then somehow they were all pushing into the house together, a rambling house, furnished anyhow, as the first glance revealed.

"Don't unpack now," Susanna was crying at them. "Come in and sit down. I want to look at you all. And I've made cookies with chocolate bits—the girls love them and I thought Peter and Lise would, too. Oh, Peter, you're grand! I did so want my Mollie to be a boy, darn her!"

She squeezed Peter in her arms and stroked his hair back from his forehead. "Malcolm, your hair used to hang over your forehead just like this—remember how Mother used to whack it off with the kitchen shears?"

"Do I!" he said.

There was a dancing gaiety about Susanna, a touch of ecstasy which he could not have explained had Corinne not done it for him.

Nadya was watching the lively woman, smiling in sympathy. Oh, Nadya was pleased with happiness and love wherever it was found, but Malcolm felt a sudden sympathy for Hartley, the brother-in-law he had never seen, for Susanna had married after he went to China. Hartley was a professor in the university nearby, a kindly man, he knew from his letters, thoughtful, inquiring, too intelligent perhaps for Susanna, but his parents had been thankful because Susanna, they always said, needed guidance.

Yet it was impossible to tell, when Hartley came in an hour later, that Susanna could possibly not love him. Indeed, Malcolm thought with some bewilderment, she obviously did love him. She ran to the door when she saw him coming up the walk, briefcase in hand, and their kiss, their embrace, were genuine. The moment he looked into Hartley's face, an honest, spectacled, good face, the moment he felt the grasp of the brown firm hand he knew that everything was genuine in this man. And so it was, he decided with further bewilderment, in Susanna, too. Could it be that Corinne was wrong? He put the puzzle aside, determined to enjoy this sister and her family, and ignoring as best he could influences within himself that he recognized as distinctly Chinese. Thus, as an elder brother, it was, after all, his responsibility to know what was going on. He had no taste for scandal. On the other hand, were Susanna not his sister, it was none of his business to know what went on in Hartley's house. Once during a vast change of regime in China he had inquired of a Chinese friend, "Will it not damage Chiang Kai-shek's reputation when, on the eve of triumph, he announces his marriage to one woman without first obtaining his divorce from three others?" The reply to this had been made promptly and with dignity. His friend, in the long blue satin robe and formal velvet jacket of a Chinese gentleman, had said in the calmest and least interested of voices, "What a man does in his own house cannot concern the nation." The reply was admirable, and then it occurred to him that it was not Hartley but Susanna, the woman, who was confusing the household and this, even in China, was quite a different confusion and far more serious.

Such thoughts, he decided with some guilt, were not to be shared with Nadya, at least not yet, and he must not mistake his own country for the one he had left forever. Meanwhile it was already pleasant to observe that his children settled easily into this hit-and-miss house, and that they loved the bright chatter of their aunt. They followed her everywhere, Lise asking questions and Peter listening, and Susanna's laughter sang through the house where all doors stood open. She was in and out of the living room, where Hartley settled himself, running in to talk and then running out again to the kitchen or to a bedroom to put more blankets on the beds, for the day, beginning so mild and soft, was turning gray and chill with evening.

"The nature of our region," Hartley said cheerfully, lighting the fire laid ready on the hearth. "The day often begins brightly and then by midafternoon the sky is gray. I suppose we are too near the sea."

"Come to supper," Susanna said after a short absence. "I haven't made a fuss—we're just having what we would have anyway."

A rustle in the hall, giggles and footsteps, made her turn her head. "Sue and Mollie, come down here!" she called. "They're so silly," she explained, turning to Malcolm. "They didn't want you to see them until they were dressed up."

"Oh, Mother!" a duet of voices, shrill and young, remonstrated, but almost immediately the girls appeared, dressed in pink frocks, their hair brushed bright and lying on their shoulders in loose curls. They looked like twins, but they were not, a year between, as Malcolm remembered.

"Sue and Mollie," Susanna said. She presented them proudly and Hartley watched, silent and amused.

"Now for heaven's sake," Susanna cried. "Let's eat before the food is ruined! I'm not a good cook, Malcolm, and it's too bad you went to Corinne's house first."

"Nonsense," Hartley said, too fondly.

These two families, commonplace and yet somehow endearing, were good enough as introduction to America. Malcolm allowed himself a week with Susanna, and marveled that never by sign or word did she reveal her secret, if indeed she had a secret. Once he suspected a telephone conversation, one evening when Hartley was late at a faculty meeting. Susanna had been listening for the phone, he imagined, for though she had been as gay as ever, he fancied that her attention was strained. When the telephone rang she hastened into the hall and then he heard the murmur of her voice, subdued beyond hearing. He looked at Nadya, caught her quizzical smile, and lifted his eyebrows. But Susanna was soon back in the room, explaining smoothly enough, "That was a call from an old friend. I was expecting it—someone just passing through town."

"I hope we aren't crowding your house," he said.

"Oh, it's no one I would invite here," she said instantly.

And this, of course, might mean nothing or much.

His children grumbled when the visit ended, and Lise, looking out of the back window of the car, made her demand: "Papá, let us buy a house exactly so like that one and live in it to be happy as they are."

He was confounded by the eternal injustice of life. Saints and sinners! He remembered that when traveling once in the far interior of a northern province in China he had come upon a fiery old missionary striding along a stone-paved street older than the streets of Jerusalem. The two white men, each of whom had thought himself solitary, stopped, stared, and then embraced each other.

"Come home with me, brother," the old missionary shouted. "The inns are full of fleas and I am the only human being in the town who doesn't eat garlic!"

He had accepted the invitation gladly and had spent the night in a vast bare mission house, listening to the overflow of that old saint.

"When I get to Heaven," the saint had proclaimed with confidence. "I am going to ask God a question—just one question, mind you!"

His lean old forefinger had wagged at Malcolm while his blue eyes burned. "I'm going to ask God why he didn't make heathens all bad and Christians all good. It would simplify the whole of human life, mind you! As it is—ha!"

"As it is?" Malcolm suggested.

"As it is," the saint declared, "there's no satisfaction in converting a heathen when you find that he was a good man anyway—none at all! And it's a humiliating thing, brother, but I'll confess it as a Christian and an honest man, and mind you"—the forefinger wagged at him again—"the two aren't always the same thing. My best Christians were once the best heathens in the town. It's no satisfaction, I tell you!"

He laughed silently to himself at the memory, and Nadya caught him and demanded her share of laughter. "Now, Malcolm, it is selfish, this habit to laugh by yourself! It is like eating a sweet in a corner with your back turned, so people cannot have it, too!"

His only answer was to laugh aloud.

II

How DOES A MAN KNOW when he has reached his bit of promised land? Here were a thousand promises, a view of mountains, shimmering blue from a knoll in a forest. Here was a small town with pleasant citizens, a new schoolhouse, a town all shining windows and green lawns, whereon the happiest children in the world ran to and fro in the maze of their games. Farms spread over the rolling hills, and clear streams rushed under steel spans or under old covered bridges. This was the landscape before his eyes one morning as they traveled northward.

"What are we looking for?" he asked Nadya. "Perhaps it would be easier to find it if we know the essentials of our home."

"Not a wooden house, please," Nadya said. "I feel the wooden house is too quick to pass. A fire, a storm— it is gone!"

71

"Most houses in America are wood," he reminded her. "It's a country of trees, Nadya."

"Ah, yes, so beautiful, as in Russia also," she agreed. "But I myself have always lived where houses are brick or stone or even beaten earth, Malcolm. I can remember once, my parents and I, we did live in an earthen house outside Peking, and it was nice, cool in summer, warm in winter."

He turned to their offspring. "Since it will be your home until you are grown up, what do you two say we must have?"

"A brook," Peter said, "and woods."

"That means not in a town," Malcolm said. "Well, I accept those conditions. Lise?"

"I like upstairs," she said eagerly. "Never did I go upstairs to live except in Aunt Corinne's house, and there I could see far. I wish a room for myself high as the trees."

Nadya put her palm on his cheek. "And you, Malcolm? Always you leave yourself last!"

"A quiet room where I can work," he said.

He had decided in these weeks that before he looked for a job, he wanted to write a book. He was not sure that he was a writer, but he wished nevertheless for six months in which to write down the book that was in him. When he had finished it he would know whether there was more in him. If not, then he would look for a job, any job, for if he were not a writer, he did not care what he was.

They discovered that day quite by accident, it seemed, and in a remote spot, a deserted house, field-stone, old, neglected. Something brave about it, a dignity of depth and roofline, caught his eye. It stood near the top of a broad hill, two trees guarded it, a sugar maple, a black walnut, and at the foot of the hill a brook ran under a three-arched bridge. He stopped abruptly.

"Well, what about it?" he inquired of his three.

"This?" Nadya exclaimed.

The children stared in silence. This their house?

"Let's get out and see," Malcolm said.

They got out and walked through knee-deep grass, they stepped on the ancient wooden porch and the double door stood open before them.

"Somebody lives here," Lise said, peering in.

In a corner of the room stood a pallet bed, a table, and an old rocking chair.

"Somebody slept here even last night," Nadya said.

Peter hung back, frightened. "It might be a bandit!"

"No bandits in America," Malcolm said heartily.

At the sound of their voices an old man came around the corner of the house. He was bent, his limbs were gnarled, and he had a swollen left cheek, a wen, Nadya thought with pity until suddenly it disappeared and lo, the wen was on his right cheek.

She gasped at this magic. "Malcolm, look, please! His wen goes from one side to the other!"

The old man grinned and showed nearly toothless gums. "It ain't no wen!" he said in a cracked voice. "It's Friday and my wad is gettin' kinda big. Tomorra I spit it out and start over again. Once a week, reg'lar——"

He spat a rich brown stream and Nadya stepped back, aghast. "Malcolm, please, what is this? Does he vomit?"

Malcolm said in haste. "My love, he chews tobacco instead of smoking it. I never thought to tell you of such things." He turned to the old man. "My wife has not been in America before."

"Furriners, are ye?" the man said amiably. The bright noon sun shone down on deep wrinkles in his face, each lined with black dirt.

"I come from Virginia," Malcolm said prudently. To say China was to be too foreign, indeed. "But we are thinking of settling in this part of the country. Is this house for sale?"

The old man looked shrewd. He took off a filthy cloth cap and scratched a filthier head. "It don't belong to me, that's a fact," he said at last. "I just live here—been livin' here for seventeen years next Christmas."

He looked up at Malcolm. "Be you folks afraid of ghoses?"

"Ghosts?" Malcolm repeated.

"Yeah, they's a ghos' here. He don't come out too often much, but ever' Christmas Eve he walks from the barn yander down to the bridge and back again. I sees him ever' year. Yeah, he's here, hidin'."

An enormous barn of stone and faded red wood stood behind the house.

"Does he come in the house?" Lise asked, her blue eyes solemn.

"Not while I'm in it, he don't," the old man said. "Devil Jack is his name, and a devil he was. He's buried in the graveyard up there in the town, but he ha'nts around here, makin' trouble. He dassent with me."

"I suppose he wouldn't with us, either, if we should buy this house," Malcolm said.

The old man looked plaintive. "I wouldn't buy this house if I was you, mister. The roof leaks any time it rains. My bed sets in the on'y dry place."

"I wouldn't put you out without seeing that you had shelter," Malcolm said, "a cabin maybe in the woods back there? Fixed up, of course?"

The shrewd little black eyes glistened. "Rent free?"

"Of course."

The old man spat again and Nadya shuddered, but he did not notice her. He pointed with a filthy forefinger down the dirt road. "Man down there kin sell it to you, but you take my advice, mister. Don't give him what he asts. He'll skin you alive. Give him half and then tell him you don't want it noways."

"Thank you," Malcolm said. Shades of China!

He led his procession to the car again and then bumped his way carefully over a road as bad as any he had ever seen anywhere.

Down the road at a farmhouse a red-faced farmer came to the gate and stared at him in silence.

"I'd like an option on the place up the road. What's the acreage?" he asked.

"Eighty," the farmer said, spitting into the dust.

"The price?"

"Five thousand."

"I'm not sure I want it, but I'd like an option for a week. How much would that be?"

"A hunnerd."

"Who's the old man there?"

"Old Yarcy. Needn't bother about him."

"Hasn't he any family?"

"No—come here when I was a kid. He works when he has to if he's got nothin' to eat, and loafs the rest of the time—steals some, I guess."

Malcolm took out his wallet and counted ten bills and asked for a receipt. The farmer went inside and stayed a long time, and came back with a few misspelled words scrawled in pencil on a piece of brown paper.

"This is Thursday—I'll be back Monday," Malcolm said.

"Suit yerself," the farmer said, spitting.

They drove away and after a silence Nadya remarked, "It is strange, is it not, Malcolm, that Americans make so much spittle? This surprises me."

"Habit," Malcolm said.

"Not only a habit," Nadya replied. "It is something shy in them. They don't know what words to speak and so they spit."

"Perhaps," Malcolm said. Let Nadya discover America as she found it!

There is no knowing why it is that one place alone pulls at the heart and speaks of home in a large country when there are scores of others better and more beautiful. During the days until Monday they drove over the surrounding hills and valleys and found other houses far more sensible for them to buy, houses finished and ready to live in, houses nearer to stores and schools. But the gallant ruined old house on the hill had clutched their imaginations. They went back to it, and this time, Yarcy not being there and all the doors open, they climbed the winding stairs and found old fireplaces with carved mantelpieces and deep windows set into the thick stone walls, an enormous attic and, downstairs again, they found a stone-floored cellar. The solitary house stood alone on a lonely hill, and the emptiness attracted them.

"As though perhaps it has been waiting for us," Nadya said.

"It will cost a great deal to make it livable," Malcolm said.

"Slowly we will do it," Nadya said.

While they talked and pondered, Peter and Lise wandered over the hill and down to the brook.

"We shall have to rip out these partitions to make rooms of a decent size," Malcolm said.

"The outside walls are so strong, so thick," Nadya said.

He supposed the matter was actually settled by his discovering behind the house another one, much smaller, a single room of stone walls and a huge fireplace, a place of cobwebs and spiders and rotting wood, but which instantly he saw as his quiet room.

"Selfishly I feel I must have this," he told Nadya.

"Then it is all ours," she said.

So it became theirs, on a Monday, as easily as possible, too easily, he feared in the night. They had no knowledge whatever of the people thereabout. They had come into a country completely strange, a wilderness for them as truly as once it had been for his forefathers, but more dangerous, for it was peopled with strangers who were his own kind. Indians had been enemies, simple and declared, the accepted targets for bullets and intrigue, but he had bought with the house neighbors unknown and unseen.

The house was a hundred and ninety-two years old. A white marble oval set into the enormous chimney announced the date. Under the date were linked initials of its first owners, man and wife. This was good, it showed a proper feeling of the man for his wife, Nadya declared.

They stood hand in hand upon the rough sod, gazing against the blue sky and the clear sunlight to look at the marble oval.

"These two, J.H. and A.H.," Nadya said. "They understood this house was not built for themselves alone. They made it for the generations."

"That was the faith of our forefathers," Malcolm said.

From within the house came such hammering and pounding and tramping of heavy feet, such loud voices of men shouting back and forth, up and down, to one another that they could scarcely hear their own voices. The children ran down the hill like rabbits every day to the brook and would not be seen again until the great iron bell, which Nadya had found hanging under the overshoot of the barn, rang for their picnic lunch under

the black walnut tree. Every day now was exactly like
every other day. They rose early in their rooms in an
ancient and nearby inn, they breakfasted upon sausage
and scrapple, scrambled eggs, strong coffee and milk,
and indigestible delicious breads. Then they drove at
once to the house. Here men were already working
and old Yarcy superintended to his own satisfaction.
Malcolm had hired him as gardener, but obviously it
was impossible to make a garden yet, and Yarcy, after
pointing this out to his employer, sat upon a broken
stone wall and directed the mason how to lay stones and
the carpenter how to pound nails. These two huge and
good-humored men listened in silence and smiled sleep-
ily. They had known old Yarcy since their somnolent
boyhoods. Somewhere in the past, their parents had
told them, there had been a Mrs. Yarcy, a slim, pretty
girl of dim wits, who had been Yarcy's humble slave.
When children were born, it seemed to the surprise of
both, she had taken a basket and gone to the kitchen
doors to beg. It had become a folktale, and children,
staring at old Yarcy's withered one-sided face, remembered the tale their mothers told, of how on any cold
winter's night there could be a knock on the door, and
when it was opened there stood the slender woman, so
pretty at first, but her blue eyes always bewildered,
and then growing thinner and more haggard as the
years passed, until the pink was gone from her cheeks
and the bewilderment in her eyes had changed to
blankness.

"There was always a baby, seemed like," any mother
would so tell the tale. "And she always said the same
thing when you ast her why didn't Yarcy provide."

"Yarcy says,"—this was whispered in the gentlest
and most pleading voice—he says can't nobody expect
him to pervide for such a many children. He says,

where'd they all come from? I don't know, myself. But they keep a-comin'."

Later, when the wild children swarmed over the hills, fishing in the streams and trapping along the banks, berrying in summer and working at a vegetable garden under old Yarcy's stern command, it was said that he beat his wife. She could be heard screaming and crying, but nobody went to see why. Old Yarcy kept a shotgun handy and even his children never told what went on in the shack of a house. It blew down finally in a strange little hurricane, shaped like a miniature cyclone, that swept across the hills one thunderous August afternoon. Mrs. Yarcy was dead by then and the children had scattered, two boys dust on a battlefield in France. Old Yarcy announced himself a free man and moved into the empty farmhouse on the hill with the last and most ferocious of his dogs. No one went near so long as the dog lived and when he died and old Yarcy was really alone, people forgot him. He was as good as dead.

Now, however, he had been resurrected. The new folks, as he called Malcolmn's family, had made him important. He was hired, their gardener, they called him, but in the nearby hamlet he said he was the manager of what was going to be an estate. He shifted his wad of tobacco vigorously from side to side, he spat copiously and described again and again how they had come, and how he had advised them against buying such a ruin and how "Malcolm"—old Yarcy stood on no formality—was a typical feller, not one of these here city fellers.

Typical, Malcolm discovered for himself, meant common, not haughty, a democratic man, in short. It was a compliment, and although Nadya was not entirely pleased that so earthy a creature as Yarcy should make himself thus free with the master, yet she could do nothing about it, certainly not after Malcolm himself pointed out to her that she was inconsistent, privately maintaining levels which she had declared were unjust.

"You are always telling me that in Russia your serfs hated you because you kept yourselves far from them. Yet here when old Yarcy calls me by my first name, which certainly he would not do if he did not like me, you are offended."

"It is the brown spittle," she said and shuddered.

"A non sequitur, my love," he retorted.

Old Yarcy at this moment was pretending not to see them. His gnarled shape had apparently collapsed upon the broken wall. He was a tangle of folded arms, crossed legs, and a hunched back. His shrunken face was lost under a large frayed straw hat, and only his jutting chin was visible, rhythmically chewing its cud.

The huge Pennsylvania Dutch carpenter stood slowly scratching his head while he contemplated the door into the house. He had taken it from its ancient hinges and laid it down upon the weedy grass. Now he stared at it doubtfully.

"What's the problem, Hank?" Malcolm asked. Hank Feldenspiegel had begged him to ignore the long and awkward family name. "Folks know I'm a Feldenspiegel when they think of it, but round here I'm just Hank—easier that way."

"This here door, mister," Hank said. "You want I should take out them two top panels for glass like you said?"

"Like I said," Malcolm agreed.

"Like you said," Hank repeated.

"Like I said," Malcolm agreed again.

After a silence and more head scratching Hank spoke.

"Sposen I find the frame is rottener than it looks to be?"

"Then we will think what to do—maybe put in a patch."

"If you say so," Hank said.

He lifted the heavy double door and shoved Yarcy gently along the wall with one end, and then put the door down upon the stones. They were uneven and Yarcy hopped off and found small stones to brace the door level. He spat, climbed on the wall again, ready to supervise the carpentry. Hank paid no more heed to him than to a sparrow. He began, his hands enormous and clumsy, yet dexterous, to loosen the panels. They came out whole, each panel two pieces of wood, face to face, dry but sound. Hank opened them and at this moment Malcolm saw words written upon the clean unpainted inner side, in heavy black pencil. He read them and shouted aloud.

"Nadya, look here!"

She was wandering through the grass, picking the long-stemmed purple violets, and hearing his voice, she came to him, her hands full of the flowers.

"Nadya, see what we've found!"

In a wondering voice she read aloud the large print-like script: "I, Joseph Hechtmann, make and work this door. April, 6, 1778. Today I marry my true love, Agnessa."

"Here's history, Nadya!" Malcolm exclaimed.

She looked up at the sturdy old house, and her eyes filled with her ever ready tears. "Oh, Malcolm, how sweet is it to find these words! They loved, too! Our house was begun with love! Oh, how happy!"

Her quick heart was in her tearful eyes, in her warm voice, in her face, soft and alive with feeling. He put his arm about her and saw old Yarcy watching them, grinning, his little black eyes shrewd and filthy.

"Found somepin?" Hank asked. He had been startled by Nadya's words and had turned to stare at her, too, but with kindly stupidity.

"Some writing here," Malcolm said abruptly.

"Most the old people did write things in old houses somewheres," Hank said.

He was staring at Nadya now, his face slowly flushing red. She caught the look, the dark and lustful look, primitive and frightening. Yarcy, too, was peering at her—Yarcy, that filthy old man!

"Malcolm!" Her voice was a whisper. She turned her head away, she clutched his arm. "Something is here like—like Russia! Serfs—looking at me—such eyes! I am afraid again!"

He laughed at her, amazed. "Nadya, you are imagining! We are at home, we are in America!"

She wavered and then was suddenly resolute. She put her hands together in the crook of his elbow and pulled him away.

"Come, Malcolm," she commanded. "Come! Let us pick violets." She pulled him along and Malcolm obeyed. Suddenly he turned. Suddenly he saw the shrewd eyes of old Yarcy and the eyes of Hank, as hot as embers. He was puzzled, strangely puzzled. But of course he was right. This was America. These men were ignorant men, doubtless, but this was America!

Under the house were deep foundations of stone, the solid stone of the fields, brown and glinted with wine red and dark gold, the same stone that made the high walls. The cellar was dry, a huge and dim cavern, lit by small sunken windows. The floor was beaten earth under the kitchen, but beneath the main house an iron cement had been laid between the stones, an old cement that had not crumbled and that gave off no dust. The vast chimney went solidly down through the house and here in the cellar spread nine feet of rock. The beams that held the floors above made the roof of the cellar, great oak beams, hewn by an ax and dark with age and festooned with cobwebs. Nadya spent hours in the cellar, a kerchief over her hair while she swept away the tough gray cobwebs undisturbed for years.

When Malcolm went down the twisting stairs to find her, she was sniffing the earthy air.

"I so like this smell," she said. "It makes me think of something I cannot remember."

He laughed. "How then can you think of it?"

"I know the smell," she insisted. "I have smelled it long ago. Maybe in my father's old house in Russia? It is the smell I remember, but not where."

They went about the vast old cellar together, exploring. Anything might be discovered where human beings had lived so long. But there was nothing except the heavy old beams, the stone walls roughly plastered, the hand-smoothed ancient cement beneath their feet. He opened the cellar door, the rusty hinges screeched, and they were out in the sunshine again.

"After all, we ought not to think our house is old," Malcolm said. "The house in Peking was six hundred years old."

"Ah, but Peking," Nadya cried. "A thousand years are but a day in its sight. Did not God say so? Whereas here, Malcolm, each year is still a century of delight. I find it so. To pick such violets everywhere upon this land now ours! I hope the days will never grow short. I hope that here everything will be the same at last, forever and forever."

He did not reply. If there were a country left upon the globe that could be the same forevermore, it must be here. If not here, then never again could it be anywhere. Here was the old faith, that faith that had inspired a certain Joseph, two hundred years ago, to write the story of his work and love upon the panel of the door he made for his house and trust that someday another man and woman would find it. As they had—as they had!

Above the cellar the rooms were already shaped. Four partitions of thick lath and plaster, strong enough to make a house, were now in heaps upon the floor. Old Yarcy was taking out loads slowly and muttering about the dust in his eyes. He had been astonished this morning when Malcolm had suggested a shovel and a basket to him as he sat perched upon the broken wall, but after staring for some minutes and chewing hard, he came down from the wall and shuffled off to find such utensils. He was extraordinarily strong. His lean withers were like ropes beneath the dry brown skin, the brown no more than dirt, for Peter had proved that Yarcy did not wash.

"Papá, I know, for I have seen upon him a certain large spot, on the side of his neck, dirt very plainly, and it is not yet off since we came here."

"I must have a shower added to the cabin," Malcolm replied. It had been done, but just now, noticing the brown spot still plain on Yarcy's skinny neck, he made it a point for question.

"How does your shower work, Yarcy?"

"I aim to try it out one of these days," Yarcy replied. "I don't dast touch water until the weather warms up."

Malcolm laughed. If Yarcy had been a man in Peking he could have said without offense, "Go away to the bath house and wash yourself clean." But in Peking it would not have been necessary. The bath was a rite. And in Peking Yarcy would have been a servant whom the master could command. Here he was a neighbor who, out of kind condescension, though for pay, was helping them out. That was what he had heard Yarcy say.

"How does it feel to have a job, Yarcy?" Thus the stonemason, newly arrived, had inquired with malice. The stonemason was a malicious little man, as anyone could see, a red-faced thin little man with a sharp, cruel sense of humor, a man to twist even a dog's tail.

Yarcy refused the implied tail twisting.

"This here ain't a real job, as you might call it. I'm just helping out a neighbor."

"You get pay for it, don't you?" So the mason reminded him.

"You might call it that," Yarcy said with dignity. "Again you mightn't. It depends on how you look at it. I don't look at it like that. If I go out for pay, it would have to be real pay that wouldn't have no idea of helpin' anybody. It's the helpin' out that makes the difference."

"It's a difference so little I can't see it," the stonemason had retorted.

With each load of debris piled into the wheelbarrow outside the door the big room began to be more plain. The stonemason was building a chimneypiece. They had gone down to the brook and found stones for it, great gold-streaked slabs that could be pried from the bedrock. Malcolm bought mallets and iron rods and he and Peter pried the slabs away while Nadya and Lise washed off the clinging moss and green slime. The stones lay now on the oaken floor ready for the mason's hand. The foundation in the cellar was wide and the mason was making the chimney as wide and deep.

"Hey, mister," he called, and Malcolm, recognizing that he was being addressed, strolled across the room. "What for shall I make the ledge?" the mason asked.

"Ledge?"

"Acrost," the mason explained. Wunnerful, he often

told his wife in the evening, how dumb smart folks could be!

Malcolm was illuminated. "Ah, a mantelpiece!"

"The ledge," the mason repeated. "Stone or wood? That's a mighty fine long piece. I could make it stone."

Nadya came and they pondered. "Stone," she decided. "Strong and never to be painted or polished."

So the stone was lifted and it stretched solidly across the vast chimney. Nothing fragile or pretty could be set there, that was plain. Possibly a pair of heavy candlesticks, iron or brass, not silver, but they must be very heavy and wide at the base.

"Does it draw?" Malcolm inquired.

"My chimneys all draws," the stonemason said with contempt.

He never looked at Nadya fully, but now and then he stole sidewise glances at her from his lashless lids, a strange, secret, lustful look, full of sin, as he well knew, for he never allowed it to linger. Nadya noticed it, however, one day. She walked away and Malcolm followed.

When he had caught up with her outside under the ancient half-dead pear tree that they could not decide to cut down and certainly not now while it was in snowy bloom, she said calmly enough, "It is my opinion, so far, Malcolm, that your American men despise women very much."

He laughed. "So far, my love, your experience is limited."

Nadya refused to laugh. "I see very clearly though not yet far. The husbands of your sisters, they are good, it is true. They do not look at other women sidewise. But they also think little of women. Ah, yes, I know."

"They were very polite to you," he reminded her.

"So polite that I knew they thought me only a woman. Do you see how the mason looks at me?"

"The stonemason is an ignorant man. I doubt he has gone to school more than a few years," Malcolm said.

"He is a good stonemason," she replied to this. "It is nothing to me that he has dirty looks at me. Yet if he did not despise all women he would not make the dirty looks."

"After all, he is only a stonemason," Malcolm said.

For the first time he felt a slight alarm. Would Nadya be lonely with her kind? Their kind, actually, for he had delighted as much as she in the friends they had made in Peking, friends of many countries—now, alas, all flown away like leaves before the bitter wind. Their houses, those charming ancient Chinese houses, furnished with Peking rugs and tables and comfortable American chairs and conveniences, those homes of cosmopolitan delight, where men and women of the world lingered for years because Peking itself was more beautiful than all other beautiful cities, what had become of them? It was beyond doubt that they still stood as they had stood through empires and revolutions before, but who lived in them now? Peasants, perhaps, at first peasants of Russia, arrogant with present power and without the knowledge of beauty, but now even Chinese peasants, whose fathers had known no better than a mud-walled hut beneath a roof of thatch. These for the moment were the strong and they were everywhere. It occurred to him that the men working on his own house a stone's throw away from him at this moment, old Yarcy, Hank, and the stonemason whose name he could scarcely remember, were brothers to them in all but blood.

It was August. The house stood ready at last, the workmen were gone, and old Yarcy was pushing a lawn mower over the tough grass, a bewildered look on his face as though he had been trapped into unaccustomed effort. The sun shone down upon the house and the clear, hot light pricked out the colors in the stone. Dark green shutters and white paint shone fresh and new, and the massive chimneys, four of them, were raised against the sky. The terrace was laid, stone upon stone, and Nadya's flower seeds, planted in May, were blooming brightly, plain country flowers, quick to grow, zinnia and petunia and candytuft.

"Home," Malcolm said.

They were standing together by common impulse in the road, still a dusty country road.

"Our home," Nadya said.

"We will live here forever," Lise declared.

Only Peter did not speak. He had grown inches during the summer. Unexpectedly he found that he liked milk and he drank it by the quart. In China the milk had been poor stuff, thin with water and always boiled. Milk? He had refused it here, too, until one day, seized by thirst near a farmhouse, he had gone in to ask for water and instead the farmer's wife had poured out ice cold milk, a tall glass of it.

"Better than water," she had said smiling at him, and in Chinese courtesy he had accepted milk instead of water, sipping it unwillingly at first and then gulping it down. This was not milk as he had known, this rich creamy liquid, tasting of the freshness of fields and the scents of flowers . . .

"Well, son?" Malcolm inquired.

"Let us go in," Peter said.

But Nadya must make a ceremony of this entrance, as she made ceremony of much of their life.

"We will not just walk in as though it were not the first time. We will make it to remember."

She went to the car and brought out a basket covered with a white napkin. This napkin she took away and beneath it was a small loaf of brown bread, a jar of coarse salt, a bottle of red wine, and a silver cup.

"Come," she said, "let us celebrate."

Together solemnly they entered the house and when they were inside the door she broke the loaf into four pieces and sprinkled salt upon each piece. She gave the bread first to Malcolm, then to Peter, then to Lise, and last to herself.

"Take it and eat," she said to each one.

Used to her solemnities, brief and intense, they took the bread in silence and ate.

"It is good bread," she told them. "I made it myself yesterday in the kitchen at the inn. Always in this house we will have good bread. I will make it."

Lise said, "Mamá, I don't like the bread at the inn. This is real bread."

Nadya instructed her daughter. "Instead of saying you don't like that, please just say you like this. It is not so nice to say you don't like something, since here is your country. We must thank God we have this country where we can make our home forever in peace and safety."

When they had eaten the bread and salt, she poured the wine into the silver cup and presented it with both hands to Malcolm.

"Drink, my love," she commanded him.

He drank, and then she presented it in the same way to Peter.

"Drink, my son."

In the same way again she said to Lise, "And drink, my daughter."

Last of all she lifted the cup to her own lips. Then she went to the great fireplace, where no fire had yet been built, and she poured out what was left of the red wine upon the stones that made the hearth.

"It is a libation," she said.

When the ceremony was over, her grave face broke into her usual sparkling smile, and she waved her hands at them.

"Come now, everybody at once, each one is to do what he likes. You, children, will want to hurry to your own rooms. See what is there—your father and I have not been idle while you roamed over the fields. And, Malcolm, you and I!"

She caught his hand while the children ran off and they ascended the stairs together. He knew where she led him. Their two rooms, adjoining, each with its own small bath, occupied the front of the house on the second floor. Unknown to the other, each had made surprises. Thus when she led him to his room, which he had supposed would be empty, he saw a large bed, the sort of bed he would exactly like, four strong posts of maple, hand-carved, and a man's chest of drawers to match, old and carefully made, and by the fireplace an easy chair with brown leather cushions.

"Nadya, what have you done?" he exclaimed. "How did you smuggle these things in?"

She brimmed with joy, she could not keep from laughter. "Yarcy helped me! I hid them in the barn, and I told him to get neighbors very early this morning and put them in. I showed him where the bed to stand, and where the chests of drawers, and the chair. Sit in the chair, Malcolm—isn't it good? Oh, to think I shall see you sitting in that chair every day, for the rest of my life! And, Malcolm, please, just stretch yourself on the bed. It is as you like, the mattress quite hard, much too hard for me, but for you perfect. And see how deep are these drawers, please, and the little one so neatly at the top, this is for handkerchiefs, this for socks, and so on, as you wish."

He obeyed that her joy might be full, and found the chair comfortable and the bed was exactly as he liked it. He took her tenderly in his arms and kissed her, a long kiss, giving her his thanks. So they stood, close together, in love, he believed, above and beyond what they had ever felt before.

But he, too, had his secrets. "Now," he said, "while you have been plotting for me, I also have had a few thoughts."

Her eyes grew big. "Malcolm!"

"I have been having some fun of my own," he went on.

He went to the door between their rooms. "Shut your eyes!"

She shut her eyes, and he led her to the door. "Now open!"

She opened her eyes and clapped her hands together. "Oh, Malcolm, no! But yes, it is—where did you find such bed?"

He had found a high old tester bed in mahogany and he had ordered a mattress and pillows such as she liked, deep and soft and satin-covered. She liked her luxuries, his Nadya, and he delighted to give them to her. She had inherited such tastes from her forebears, and not all the hardships of refugee life in Manchuria and Peking had driven out of her the love of fine stuffs and beautiful objects. A graceful bureau, which had come from an English country house, he had found in a Philadelphia shop, a rosewood sewing table, a blue velvet chair.

It was too much for her. She turned and buried her face against his breast and wept. "I do not know why I am given the grace of God to be your wife!"

He reproached her with love and tried to make her laugh. "You are so beautiful, Nadya—irresistible!"

She lifted her wet lashes. "Hundreds of girls were in Peking much more beautiful than was I! You know it, Malcolm. You remember very well Cerise, with the

black hair and black eyes big like this"—she made circles with her fingers—"and such white skin, and ter-
ribly loving you! Really! And I did not dare to tell her
when you asked me to marry you. She might kill me,
or herself—or you!"

This made him laugh sincerely. But he liked it, too.
He was honest enough to admit that it was pleasant to
think that beautiful women in Peking had yearned over
him. Thus, half ashamed that he was pleased, he gave
Nadya a little push.

"Now, my dear, stop your nonsense. And get to work
please, madame housewife. If you need me, then call
me. I shall be in my study."

Yarcy, seeing him come out of the house alone and
cross the terrace to the study, felt it gave occasion for
a rest and he followed.

"This yere study," he said, at Malcolm's heels, "was
the summer kitchen. Come dog days, wimmin didn't
want to light the stove in the kitchen. It het the house
up terrible. So they'd come out yere and cook over the
fire coals."

Yarcy had discovered cunningly that if he produced
fragments of history, the doings of old times, he could
delay discussion of present tasks about the place. The
new folks were always ready to listen to what the old
folks used to do. He entered the wide chimney fireplace, high enough for him to stand in, and pointed up
the chimney.

"Look in yere, Malcolm," he commanded.

Malcolm stooped and looked in and saw a rectangle
of blue sky above.

"I'll gerrantee that up yander somewhere in this yere
chimney there be a stone loose. Inside there's mebbe a
tin box, mebbe money, mebbe writin's. That's where
the old folks use to hide things."

"I should think the fire would burn them," Malcolm said, unbelieving.

"Not through stone like thisyere," Yarcy said.

"Didn't you ever climb up and see?" Malcolm suggested.

"Don't keer enough about sech things," Yarcy said cheerfully. He was about to spit and then remembered himself. It was unfortunate, but he had to go outside. Even he knew now that he must not spit on clean hearthstones and a polished floor.

He shifted his wad. "Only thing I feel kinda bad about," he said sadly. "Thisyere old oak floor—it must be a hundred or two years old! If I was you, I'd lay down a linoleum over it. It would look real nice thataway."

"I'll think about it," Malcolm said, repressing a shudder.

Old Yarcy paused at the door. "And them rough old beams you left thataway in the house, oak they be, too. But you could cover 'em easy. Lath and plaster and a nice paper job would do it."

"Thanks for the hint," Malcolm said.

Yarcy could make no reply. Drowning in spittle, he hastened outdoors, and after an interval the lawn mower began to drone.

Malcolm shut the heavy old door. This room was wholly his own. In Peking he had had his offices, handsome rooms furnished by the United States government, belonging to him while he was employed there. But this was his own. He had no employer now except himself. Here he would do his real work. First of all, at that desk, he would write the history of the years in a country now lost to him. It would be more than a report to the State Department. It would be the whole truth about all he had learned in the years. He had gone to China a young man and he had returned with youth gone. Now in his maturity, with wisdom if ever he was to attain wisdom, free at last to say what he wished, free in a free country, he would write all he knew, that he might be of use in his generation.

He sat down on the deep windowsill and gave himself over to thought. A grim generation, his, but his son's would be yet more grim if the wisdom of the father were not enough for understanding. A few more years Peter had—the difference between thirteen and eighteen was pitifully small. He would still be a child. Yet years before manhood, he might have to bear the burden of the future, unless his father could prevent it by wisdom and by wisdom alone.

"God help me," Malcolm muttered suddenly and was amazed at the instinctive words. It had been a long time since he had called upon God for help, not since as a boy of twelve he had tried to save his best friend from drowning. Why should he remember what so long he had forgot? They had decided one day in May, the two boys—and he could remember Tom's face as clearly as though he stood here, a nondescript, ordinary boy's face—they had decided to stop on the way home from school to go swimming. It had been a hot, breathless day and school had been intolerable. The thought of water was heavenly and to the swimming hole they had gone. Stark naked, they had stayed an hour in the water, more than an hour, maybe, and then conscience stung, had been about to climb out. But Tom always wanted one more dive. One more dive and he did not come up, and after waiting too long, he had dived after his friend. Down under the muddy water he had called upon God.

"Help me to find Tom, O God!"

But Tom by wild chance had dived between the branches of a hidden tree, and the force of his dive had impelled his head into a crotch from which he could not pull himself. When Malcolm found him it was too late. He could not pull the limp body from the trap. He had been compelled to come up himself for air and then forgetting his nakedness, he had raced to the nearest house . . .

He got up abruptly from the windowsill. What tricks memory could play, and how useless it was to remember now that futile prayer!

Peter had chosen this room. When they were choosing, this was the one for him, the attic room in the wing. It was large, almost square, and the chimney from the huge fireplace in the kitchen below, where the older people had cooked their meals, was built straight up through the oaken floor to make a smaller fireplace for him. The chimney narrowed but it was still five feet wide. The room stretched across the house, so that two windows faced south and two north. Lise's room was in the attic above the rooms his father and mother had chosen. The reason he had wanted this room the moment he saw it was because he could be alone here, really alone, no Lise above him and no father and mother in the rooms below. A separate small winding stair ran into a little back hall, the entrance to the kitchen, and in the mornings when he got up early he could go outside and no one would know it. The room was cut off from the other rooms upstairs by a passage, too narrow to be a hall, and at one end of this was a small bathroom, his own. He had asked for bookshelves along the walls under the windows, and they were there. They were empty now but he would fill them. He saw rows of books ready to be read and reread, books he could never get in Peking. He had learned French early from his mother and then later he had perfected himself because the only good bookshop in Peking belonged to a Frenchman and the books were in French, but he preferred English, only he wished, now that he was going to be American, that the Americans had their own language and that he could learn it and so be altogether American.

When could he begin to be American and how? This house was home, that he had already begun to feel, the home of his family, and while he loved the woods and the brook, America was somewhere beyond the house and the land. Other boys lived in the houses he had passed in the car, the houses clustered in the village and the small town where was the inn. He had looked at the boys from afar, passing them on the street and seeing them sometimes, too, when he went to the cinema, which now must be called motion pictures, or even movies. The girl at the desk at the inn asked him on Saturdays, "Ain't you goin' to the movies? There's a good one tonight."

He had gone a few times and had watched not so much the screen but the boys of his own age, swaggering, sauntering, sometimes in gangs, sometimes alone with a girl. When a boy was alone with a girl he was surprised and disgusted, by the way they behaved, the embracing, the kissing. He could not imagine himself alone with a girl, and therefore he must think of himself with a gang of boys, all chewing gum, which his mother had forbidden him to do. If it became necessary for him to chew gum in order to maintain friendship, he would be compelled to ask her not to forbid it.

"Peter!"

His mother's voice sang up the stairs.

"Yes, Mamá?"

"Sheets, Peter, pillowcases, towels, all for you! I will come soon to help you."

He had never made a bed in his life but he understood that in America it was necessary to learn such tasks. He went soberly to find her, and there she was in the upper hall, her arms full of the linen.

"I come now," she said, and he could see from her eyes that she was happy, and indeed from her whole look he could see it. She walked in, smiled, and pushed him playfully with her shoulder.

"Come on, American boy! Anyway, I can teach you how to make your bed."

She was very particular about it, exacting firm corners and ends well tucked in. The counterpane was blue, the same stuff as the curtains, and he had chosen it, as he had chosen the furniture, strong maple wood, newly made. He had no liking for the old things his parents wanted. He wanted strong new things that nobody had ever used before, a bed for him, the mattress fresh and unyielding.

When the bed was made his mother paused.

"You like this room, Peter?"

"Very much, Mamá."

"I hope you are very happy here."

He saw her eyes brim with tears and turned away from the sight. She cried easily, and he did, too. When he saw her eyes brim like that, a sob trembled in his own breast. He wished that she wouldn't cry when she felt excited or happy or sad. It made him uncertain, as though life wasn't going to be as good as he wanted it to be because maybe underneath everything there was sadness. That he did not want to believe and he would not believe it.

"Of course I shall be happy, Mamá," he said.

Lise had done nothing at all in her room. She had settled into the deep little seat in the gable window and sat gazing over the rolling hills. They were not high hills, and she was glad for that. The hills around Peking had been high, but not wooded. These hills looked furry with trees, and the shadows were not clear blue and black upon them as they were on the Chinese hills.

"Lise!" Her mother's voice floated up the winding stairs.

"Yes, Mamá?"

"Have you made your bed, my child?"

"No, Mamá."

"Then what are you doing, my dear?"

"Nothing, Mamá."

"Oh, Lise, such a busy day you are doing nothing at all?"

"Mamá, I don't know how to make my bed."

"I will come."

She heard her mother's light footsteps running up the stairs, and she made haste to the bed and began to unfold the sheets. She had chosen a canopy bed, an old-fashioned one, because she imagined the moment she saw it how cozy it would be at night to sleep under the flowery roof. Under it she would not be afraid of the thunderstorms, the frightful American thunders and lightnings that did really kill people sometimes. Only a few weeks ago a man on the next farm had been killed, old Yarcy told them. The man had gone out with a metal bucket in his hand to take water to his fowls, as her mother called them, though they were only chickens—hens and cocks, that is—and the lightning had reached down a long silver spear from the sky and had struck him in the heart. In China there was no such lightning. She had never heard of a man or woman or even a child being so killed. Therefore as soon as she saw the canopy bed, she had wanted it, because under the ruffled canopy she could be safe from the lightning. When the thunder roared she could get into her bed and be safe.

"Now," her mother said, a little breathless from the stairs. "Please you will be careful to make the corners nice. So——"

Her mother lifted the corner of the mattress and

folded the end of the sheet left and right and Lise tried to do the same.

"You must learn here how to do such work," her mother said in her pleasant voice. "You remember how your auntie Corinne and your auntie Susanna do such work nicely, not complaining too much. So also must you and I."

"Are we poor now?" Lise asked.

"Not poor and not rich," her mother said. "But Papá wishes to write some books, and so we are a little poor until he finishes them. But it is not just poorness, dear. It is necessary that we live as do others, and not some special way. In Peking we lived like Chinese, with many servants, here we live like Americans with machines. I must acquaint myself with the machines when the bed is made."

This was soon, she was gone, and Lise was alone again, sitting on the window seat, gazing over the hills.

The machines! This was Nadya's secret. She woke in the night and thought of them with doubt and fear and in the morning she delayed their use. She must not ask Malcolm to help her. He had his own work to do. It was she who must make the machines work. But could she do so? The carpet sweeper, for example only, something with a long rope, the end of which must be attached to the wall—she went to the closet now while she was alone and opened the door and there it was, bright, new, strong, willful. It looked very willful. She knew, for the man who brought it had told her, that when the rope was in the wall, she must also press the metal bit here. She touched the metal bit carefully, then pressed it down. The machine did nothing, it remained silent, ignoring her. Then she remembered. She had not put the end of the rope in the wall.

She pulled the machine out on its little wheels and

pushed it into the living room, where some shreds of excelsior remained on the rug from a box of china that she had unpacked. Now she put the end of the rope to the wall and it fitted exactly into a socket. From this socket it sucked up the nourishment of electricity which gave it strength. This could be understood. Now was the time to press the metal bit. She did so and was instantly half stunned by the roar she heard from the machine. Quickly she shut it off. It would never do. She could not manage this creature. She sat down on the sofa, the new cherry red sofa, and lit a cigarette, her hand trembling. She must collect herself, perhaps read something from one of the magazines Malcolm had only this morning bought, so that the low table would look used, homelike, and so on. But she could not concentrate, although the pictures were bright and beautiful foods in dishes, rooms all new and clean. Clean? It was necessary to keep houses clean, and she must keep hers also.

She longed to call out, as she would have done in Peking, "Yien Er, come and sweep, please!" Yien Er was the houseboy and he would have come quickly with a short-handled broom and one of the tin dustpans which he made so cleverly from oil cans. But Yien Er was far beyond the call of her voice, perhaps even now, poor soul, in a Communist jail, because he had insisted upon staying with the family until the end.

Tears filled her eyes but she hardened herself. This was not Peking. This was America, and she must become an American woman. She rose, summoned her strength, put out the cigarette, and approached the machine again. It stood stubbornly as she had left it. All this time while she had been sitting on the sofa, the creature had been sucking its nourishment. Would this not make it more noisy than ever? She set her teeth and pressed the handle. The roar was only the same as before, and she stood, letting it roar. But the machine was impatient to move, it trembled and inched itself along, and so she took the handle firmly in both hands. Then it began to move, pulling her with it, she imagined. Nevertheless, her face very flushed, she managed to guide it up and down while it breathed in the scraps of excelsior. She had to confess that it did this. But so much was enough for the first day. It was not necessary to guide the machine over the entire room. A little more tomorrow, perhaps, but today merely acquaintance was all that she could manage. She pulled the rope from the wall and a small flame flew out, further to terrify her. Was this correct, that fire should flame from the wall of their house? She repressed her desire to fly to Malcolm. No, without nourishment the machine was quite helpless. She pressed the metal bit, but there was no roar. The creature was dead and she pushed it back into the corner and shut the door. She would say nothing to him about it.

At the table an hour later, their first midday meal, for which she had plucked a small bouquet of flowers before she served the broiled beef, sliced thin, the salad, the baked potatoes, Malcolm said, "How did things go for you, Nadya?"

"Oh, excellent, thank you, Malcolm," she replied instantly. She looked at him, her blue eyes cloudless, and was pleased to see that he believed her. The machine was safe in the closet and tomorrow when he was in his quiet room, she would take it out again and this time she would not first sit for a long time on the sofa. No, the machine should not be master.

Thus they learned how to live in their house, each in his own room with his own thoughts, and then together in the whole house. A new kind of life began here, entirely different from any they had ever known. It was very quiet. Except for the coming and going of old Yarcy, tramping into the kitchen for a drink of water as an excuse to see what they were doing, the house might have been in an empty continent. No walls stood about the house, such walls as had enclosed the house in Peking, but none were needed, for no one came near. Nor were there such sounds as had floated above those distant walls, the musical calls of vendors of fruits and flowers and sweets, the cries of children, the quarrels of ricksha pullers, the screams of women angry against their husbands or with each other, the piercing wail of a mother searching for the wandering soul of her dying child. All these sounds had been the voices of life in the Peking house. But here there were no human sounds except their own voices calling each to the other. Birdsong and the rising wind in the pines on the hill made the quiet more deep.

Were they lonely, Malcolm wondered? Not he, for in the silence of his study he shut all doors, and he wrote slowly and easily, although without knowledge of whether what he wrote was good or could interest another. It was a cleansing process. He rid himself of wastes accumulated in his memory, he clarified the past, retaining for the future only what was of significance. He had no wish, as yet, to discover friends.

Was Nadya lonely? He thought not. She was still learning how to live in the house. She had a coordinating eye, a sense of ensemble, she could imagine how a room must look and then shape it to design and she loved the task. She was a woman complete in herself, she had experience in life and love, and nothing more was necessary, or so he felt. Besides, was he not here?

Of the children he was far less sure and it was for them he felt concern. They had been wrenched from their world. Conceived in love, they had grown up tender, and the Chinese, for all their naturalism, their crass poverty and crass riches, were tenderhearted. They had given abundant love and admiration to the two fair children. The servants in the Peking house had adored them from birth and as soon as Peter and Lise could walk they had led them proudly into the streets to show to the whole city, as they thought, the beauty of these Western children with milk-white skin. How would Peter and Lise find their own reality in a country in which they now had no special place, since there were thousands like them? Old Yarcy already did not conceal his contempt for a boy thirteen years old who had never handled a hoe or a spade, and who did not know work when he saw it. Malcolm was compelled to acknowledge that Peter, his son, did not imagine it his duty to take part in the care of house or grounds. This, as he very well knew from the memories of his own youth, would never do for an American man. True, those memories had been overlaid by years when he, too, had no duty toward any form of manual labor, for in Peking the cheap and willing servants would have been shocked and even reproachful had the master of the house taken an implement in his hands more heavy than his own pen.

And Lise, where would she find the girls she needed at this age as bosom friends with whom to exchange confidences and laughter? And she, too, had already asked why she must do the work of servants in the house.

When such thoughts beset him he grew restless, he was unable to work, and responsibilities he had never faced until now made him get up from his chair and pace the wide old boards of the floor between fireplace and wall. He had stayed too long away from his own country. The years in Peking had been easy and beautiful. Encompassed by many wars in centuries past, the city had been spared because no conqueror could fail to love its space and proportion, its profound history and present grace. It stood intact, he did not doubt, the porcelain roofs of the temples royal blue and the old palaces imperial yellow, the color of the golden dragon—that vanquished dragon! And vermilion, the bright vermilion of the gates and altars, created the final trinity of color. When he remembered Peking he forgot where he was and he forgot wife and children and he sat down again to write.

"The Chinese, through centuries of varying government, have nevertheless clung to the divine right of the people to rebel. The right of kings and emperors to rule is considered not given by God, or Heaven, but by a contented people——"

"Lise," Peter said, "are you afraid?"

They were in the woods where the brook curved around an island of its own making. After a thunderstorm and a rain as heavy as typhoon rain, the brook swelled until the island became a small and lonely peak under an old willow tree, surrounded by water as muddy as the Yangtse River. Today was fine, there was no flood, and the children sat under the willow tree, their bare feet in the rippling water. This was brown earth country, the very rocks were brown, though flecked with gold, which shone under the water where the sun fell through the tree.

"Afraid of what?" Lise asked with caution.

"Of beginning," Peter said.

"Beginning what?" she persisted. Peter never finished what he meant and she took pleasure in making him finish.

"School, other boys and girls who don't know us."

"We should also go to church when we start school," Lise said.

"Why church?" Peter inquired.

"Mamá says here we must do everything others do," she replied.

"We didn't in Peking."

"We were special there and so we could do what we liked. But here we are not special, and so we must do what others do, or they will laugh at us."

"Will they?"

"Perhaps."

"Did Mamá say so?"

"She says always it is better to do what they do."

"Even church?"

"She did not yet say church, Peter. This is my thinking."

A red squirrel sat on its haunches to stare at them and they were instantly silent. Never before had they lived where small wild animals lived, and this made the woods a fairy place.

Lise was sensible. She said, when the squirrel was gone, "Let us wait and see what people do. Perhaps everything will be quite easy and pleasant, even to go to the church."

They spoke a mixture of English and Chinese when they were alone together, although in the presence of their parents they already pretended that they had forgotten their Chinese and by no coaxing could old Yarcy persuade them to let him hear how "heathen" Chinese talked. Alone they spoke all important words in Chinese, in order that meaning could be exactly expressed.

Peter did not answer, and when Lise saw him silent, and when she saw him pushing his toes into the crevices of the brown rocks under the water, she decided that he was afraid. But she did not accuse him. She had learned many things in Peking, and among them was consideration. This her old nurse had taught her, a wrinkled woman already a great-grandmother, whose feet had been bound when she was a child. To her Lise had said one day, "Ah, your feet are ugly, Liu Ma! I am glad my feet are not like yours."

To which the Chinese woman had replied, "They are ugly but it is beneath you to say so. Only stupid people wound others. Wise people are always kind."

Peter was afraid, but she, Lise, was not stupid and she would not say so. Instead she felt suddenly tender toward him.

"I wish I had such long toes as you," she said. "Mine are stubby, are they not?"

He glanced at her feet carelessly. "It doesn't matter, does it?"

"I dislike stubby toes," she said. She was eager to comfort him with praise and she went further even for this. "Really, my feet look as if they had been bound, like Liu Ma's!"

Nadya continued to make her own bread. In the kitchen alone she kneaded her bread into great swelling loaves. She looked up at the noise of a motor one morning, and she saw a truck draw near to the door, a green truck, bearing in large white letters the name MAX YANDER, and beneath them in smaller leatters BREAD PIES CAKES. A man got out and came to the open door, staring at her as if he had never seen a woman kneading bread before.

"Good morning, ma'am," he said. He took off a yellow cloth cap. "I heard you folks had moved in and I was wonderin' if you wanted bread."

"Good morning," Nadya said. "You see I make my own."

"A lot of trouble, ain't it?"

Nadya, too, could not wound. "We are so used to our own bread," she said coaxingly. She was surprised to see a sudden admiration in the man's eyes, which she very well recognized. In the lonely years before she met

Malcolm, she had been a spectacular figure in Peking, a young girl, tall, slender, shiningly blond, coming and going to her classes. Tourists, lonely white men traveling eastward from the wilds of Mongolia, foreign tradesmen from Shanghai and Tientsin in Peking for a holiday, had been impelled to stare at her and then to speak to her. She knew just the right coolness to put into her voice.

"Thank you for stopping by, just the same." She was very busy now, rolling and pressing the air from the dough. The bubbles snapped and the soft mass grew smooth. The man lingered.

"You folks plannin' to stay here?"

"Oh yes, this is our home now."

"You come from somewhere far away, I hear."

"Yes, from China."

"I've heard of it, but I never seen no Chinese before."

"We are not Chinese," Nadya said.

"I thought you wasn't, maybe, but I didn't know for sure."

"No, I am Russian, actually, and my husband is American."

The man still stared at her, but the look she recognized faded from his eyes. Another look was there, which she did not know.

"Well, I'll be goin' along," he said hastily.

"Goodbye," she called after him.

Out in the yard she saw him stop and talk with Yarcy, a long slow talk, the man chewing a stalk of grass and Yarcy leaning on his spade and spitting brown juice. Then she saw Malcolm come out from his study. It was midmorning and sometimes he came over to get a drink of water or a piece of fruit or merely to see what she did. He stopped to speak to the strange man, she saw him smile and after a moment grow grave, very grave. He began to talk with energy and even vehemence. The man listened, staring at him.

When he came in the house she had the loaves in their tins and set aside to rise again for baking. Malcolm shut the door behind him.

"Nadya," he said abruptly, "did you tell that man you were Russian?"

Her hands were still dusty with flour. "I am, so why not?"

"He does not understand that you are White Russian. He doesn't understand anything, I am afraid."

"Then he had better to know," she said, her voice very firm.

"Nadya, listen," Malcolm said. "Please don't tell anyone that you are Russian! Believe me—it is better not."

"Why, Malcolm?"

"They don't understand the difference between White and Red."

"Then it is better they do understand."

"Darling, don't get angry. They will understand after a while, but not at first, when we have just come."

She was washing her hands very carefully, examining her nails, not looking at him. "How can I live, Malcolm, trying to hide what I am? I am not one to hide. I love Russia, though I am not Communist. It is I who do not understand why they cannot know this simple truth."

"Then trust me, Nadya. Let *me* explain to people. It is not something to hide, but only to explain."

She struggled with sudden tears and then smiled. "Very well, Malcolm. To that I can agree. Please kiss me."

He took her in his arms. "It will be all right," he promised her, and he kissed her to seal the promise.

"Kiss—kiss—kiss," old Yarcy said, "that's all them two do."

He jerked his chin toward the closed kitchen door. "Betcha if you looked in at thatyere window, you'd see 'em kissin'."

Max Yander giggled. "Haven't they two big kids?"

"Yeah, but they don't think of that," old Yarcy said contemptuously. "They're queer."

"All furriners are queer," Max said.

"Yeah, I believe it," old Yarcy said.

Both men longed to continue pleasant talk on a warm bright morning, but Max had a route which he must complete, a certain number of customers, if he were not to have stale bread on his hands, and he felt compelled to duty.

"Well, so long," he said.

"So long," Yarcy said. He waited until the man was twenty feet away and then yelled after him, "Have you got any of them saucer pies?"

Max stopped. "Cherry and apple."

"Gimme one of each."

The transaction took fifteen minutes, and old Yarcy was another fifteen minutes eating the pies. He glanced at the kitchen window and then at the zenith. Noon was not more than an hour away, and it wouldn't hurt to rest. Anyways, if they said anything, he could quit and tell 'em to get somebody else. A man could always quit. After the pies he felt sleepy and he put his spade on his shoulder under the pretense that he would work a while in the vegetable garden instead of the flower border. Once out of sight, he curled behind a pine tree and went to sleep.

Max Yander continued his way. His mind pursued two streams of thought as he maintained a steady pace of fifty miles an hour. He tried to plan how he could make enough money to buy a car and he wondered whether his wife Shirley Louise would be nice to him tonight. These were the two alternatives of his habitual thought. If he was not thinking of sex he was thinking of money, except for brief seasons when he took an interest in annual football and baseball scores. This morning, the air being so warm and still, sex was uppermost, always quivering and ready, but stimulated now by the thought of those two in the kitchen, kissing, though they were man and wife. He wished that Shirley Louise was like that foreign woman. Shirley Louise was a blonde, too, somehow he couldn't go for brunettes, a redhead maybe but not brunettes, but Shirley Louise wasn't as easy as he wished she was. What else did a man marry for except to have a woman right there when he felt like it? Kissing in the kitchen! Shirley Louise wouldn't stand for it—not real kissing. It had to be night and dark and upstairs in their bedroom with the door locked, because the kids were getting so big. If he had a car now, she might be nicer. Imagining this possibility, he could not control the impulse to take an hour out of the morning and go home.

Shirley Louise was in the kitchen, too. She was surprised to see him and detecting the all too familiar glance in his eyes, she was not pleased. This was the sort of thing he used to do when they were first married, but she thought she'd broken him of it.

"What're *you* doing here?" she inquired, accenting the pronoun heavily.

"I've got a headache," he lied. "Thought I'd stop by for an aspirin."

But he could not resist fondling her breasts as he passed and she pushed him away. "Cut that out, Max! Ain't you ashamed, right in broad daylight, in the kitchen, too? What do you think I am?"

"You're my wife, ain't you?"

She glared at him, her hands on her hips, a thin blond slip of a woman, brittle and tense. "If you'd lay off for a while, so's we don't have another kid, we could buy a car."

He tried to laugh. "Guess we're not up to tricks!"

She refused to laugh. "Get back to your job, Max! I'm goin' to scrub the kitchen floor."

He had to go upstairs to get the aspirin he did not need.

"Malcolm?"

Nadya's voice was subdued to the atmosphere she deemed necessary, or at least respectful, for the creation of a book.

He looked up. She stood in the doorway, the sun shining through her hair. She was letting it grow again, and it was long enough to tie back with a blue ribbon for a chignon, he noticed irrelevantly, for surely there had been plenty of other times before now to notice such a thing.

"A priest is come, Malcolm," Nadya said.

"A priest?"

She hesitated before his incredulity. "Not Buddhist, not Catholic, it is not so plain, but he looks a priest in a black coat and small white collar."

"What does he want?"

"He has a church, he says to me, and will we come to it? What shall I tell him?"

Malcolm sighed. He had a moment before penned these words: "Communism in China began, as a matter of history, many decades before the Second World War. It had its source in the despair of the revolutionist Sun Yat-sen, when, unable to interest the Western powers in his revolutionary plans, he turned to Soviet Russia for help. It was an act as dangerous as though the shepherd called upon the wolf to help him herd his willful sheep."

The lines were the introduction to what he planned

as a closely reasoned survey of the modern Chinese revolution. But he had made up his mind some weeks ago, when Nadya had been bewildered by a Fuller brush man into buying a number of articles which she did not in the least understand, that he would come when she called. A minister could be perhaps even more bewildering than a Fuller brush man, since he had more significant but less concrete goods to sell.

He crossed the terrace to the living room door, which was open to the warm sun. Two copper-colored cocker spaniels he had bought for the children lay on the threshold like a heavy door mat and he stepped over them. Inside the big shadowy room under the dark beams a tall sandy-haired young man stood by the fireplace, his hands in his pockets as he stared at the painting over the mantelpiece.

He turned at Malcolm's footstep. "Mr. MacNeil?"

"Yes."

They shook hands. "I am Owen Hastings, minister at the Lutheran Church in the next town."

"Sit down," Malcolm said.

The young man hesitated. "This is an extraordinary painting—what is it?"

"T'ang pottery horses," Malcolm said. "I wanted all the time I was in China to own a pair of them, but the good ones are beyond any purse like mine. A young Chinese painter copied these from a pair in the museum in Peking and gave the picture to me as a parting gift. Rather symbolic, I thought, as though he said, 'Remember China as she was, not as she is now.' The T'ang dynasty, you know, was the very high height of Chinese civilization, the period of greatest freedom and therefore of greatest artistic achievement—the two always go together, of course."

"I don't know anything about China," the young

minister said. "I was a chaplain in the Pacific during the war, but we never got into China."

He sat down, his eyes on the painting, still puzzling.

Malcolm explained. "The figures on the horses are women polo players, and the horses themselves are the stubby-tailed, strong-backed Mongol ponies that you still see in North China."

"Polo players—women?"

Malcolm laughed. "Polo came from Mongolia, I believe, and the women there are a strong, independent breed—though these look rather delicate, I grant you. But perhaps they were ladies of high birth, as indeed they must have been to play polo—the game of kings, isn't it called? Queens, in this case! At any rate, since pottery T'ang horses are grave objects they were probably buried with the ladies. Perhaps these were two sisters who fell from their horses in an exciting game and were killed."

The young minister listened, entranced. "It's another world, isn't it?"

"Ah," Malcolm said, "so it seems to us here."

"You mean it's strange to you here?"

"Not for me—but for my wife and children, yes."

"I hope you will come to my church and find friends."

The two men looked at each other, half embarrassed, half friendly. "We're not very religious in the usual sense," Malcolm said. "My wife is a White Russian and her people were Orthodox Greek Catholic, when they fled their country into exile, but they gave it up. My people were Presbyterian, but I was never a practicing member."

"My church will be the right place for you," the minister said. "We don't ask what people have been—only what they are."

"Perhaps we'll have to find out what we are," Malcolm said. He did not want to commit himself. Still, there was something very winning about this tall fairhaired young man.

"This house is charming," Owen Hastings said. "We have only seen it as a lonely deserted old place as we passed. My wife Mary said the other day that it is a pleasure now to look at. It took imagination, she said."

"Well, my wife is full of that," Malcolm replied easily. "Actually there wasn't much to do. The proportions were here. Proportion is the one basic element, I suppose, in almost anything." He smiled. "I'm not sure whether that's true or whether it only seems true because I have lived so many years in China."

He could see he was somewhat beyond the young minister's depth. Proportion was perhaps not exactly the subject to discuss with a man whose life was based on one religion. But he liked the honest effort in the young man's rather simple and certainly handsome face. "I'll tell you what we'll do," he said, "we'll talk it over, parents and children, and let you know. I rather think we'll come to your church, if we come to any."

"Thanks," Owen Hastings said. "That's fair of you."

He got up, oppressed suddenly with the remembrance of other calls much less pleasant, to which he must attend. He had a mixed parish, rich and poor, city people who had moved to this region near enough to business to live in, workers in small factories for hosiery and men's pants, a few farmers, some storekeepers, and many schoolteachers. They had only one element in common, as he told Mary, when they were discussing the perennial problems of the church members. They had all once been something else.

But he was young and full of idealism. His roots were not deep, for he was not a scholar. He had been rather a wild young man, the only son of good parents, god-fearing, he put it. In the army he had done nearly everything he should not have done, as well as much that he should have done and had indeed been compelled to do. He had never thought of death until the sight of his mates, young men like himself, destroyed before his eyes, had forced him to consider what he was. He made a vow to a God he did not know, that if he lived he would become a minister. He was not superstitious, but the fact was that he had miraculously escaped death more than once after that, and so he had kept his vow.

He reached the small brown stone manse in time for luncheon with his wife and while they ate their somewhat too hearty meal, for they had healthy bodies and good appetites, he told her about the new people on the hill.

"They're not queer," he said, "but certainly they are different. I didn't see the children. The parents are stunning, though, Mary. He's tall and dark, and she is tall and blond."

"Old?" Mary inquired.

"No," Owen hesitated, considering. "They're the age that you don't think of as young or old. I can't imagine them ever being either, somehow."

Mary herself was very young, young and pretty and a member of the Junior League in New York, and deeply in love with her young husband. When she went to New York she joked about her country parson of a husband and about being a parson's wife, and it all seemed a merry sort of life which she could leave if she did not like it, for of course Owen could get a big church if he wished, or her father would take him into the banking business. Meanwhile her mother paid for a maid, because of course Mary had to have help.

"If the new people aren't young," she said, "then they're old, too old for us, anyway."

Her face, sharply pretty, was suddenly dimmed by discontent.

The leaves were turning gold and crimson and a warm nut-brown. The schoolroom was cold and Mrs. Heller, the teacher, lit the iron stove. Lise's desk was near it, and soon the heat began to rise and wrap her in warmth, a pleasant, not too violent heat of burning wood, "light wood" Mrs. Heller called it because the heavy wood was saved for the winter. The grade school children still stayed in one-room schoolhouses, but Peter, who was in junior high, went to a big consolidated school in the county seat. Lise was glad that she could stay here in a cozy small room with everyone together, the ten fifth-graders and the fifteen fourth-graders, and Mrs. Heller to teach them one after the other, the quick ones helping the slow ones and the fifth-graders helping the fourth-graders. At first she had felt strange, but now the room seemed almost like another home, to which she came in the morning to spend the day. To spend the day was the way to put it, for it was a pleasant day, and sometimes she felt sleepy and she put her head down on the desk and slept, and Mrs. Heller did not waken her. She read and she studied, and sometimes she whispered with Mary Ellen, who sat behind her and was now her best friend. It was sweet to have a best friend, someone who taught her how to speak American English and not the English her mother knew, someone who in recess combed her hair and made it look American. She had a friend, a best friend.

"Do you know who my best friend is?" she asked her mother.

"Who, darling?" Nadya asked.

"Mary Ellen."

"Mary Ellen and what else?"

"I don't know—just Mary Ellen."

"Ask her the last name also," Nadya said, "so that I may know if I meet the mother in the grocery store."

"Lise is very advanced," Mrs. Heller wrote primly on Lise's report card. "Her travels have given her an advantage. But she needs to learn how to study. She is too restless."

"What is restless?" Nadya asked her daughter.

"I don't know, Mamá." Lise said.

"Ask your teacher," Nadya told her child. "What you don't know you must find out with questions."

"Here nobody asks questions, Mamá," Lise said.

"Then you alone must ask," Nadya said firmly.

"What is *restless*, Mrs. Heller?" Lise asked the next day.

"It means to move around too much, Lise," Mrs. Heller said in her kind voice. "It means to get up and walk about, to whisper, to wriggle at your desk. Yesterday you dropped your book four times and every time all the children in the both grades stopped their work to look at you."

"So why are you restless?" Nadya asked when Lise had reported what Mrs. Heller said.

"Because I am always moving inside myself," Lise said literally.

"This cannot be," Nadya said. "You have traveled too much, but now we travel no more. We are here. We shall go nowhere else. Now we are like trees, not birds. The birds fly hither and thither, but the tree puts down long deep roots and even the wind cannot pull it up. When you sit in your desk say to yourself, I am a tree. I put down my long deep roots and I am still."

At her desk Lise tried to think she was a tree putting down her roots. She thought of the earth and the roots going down into the rock and the clay. For a day she was not so restless and that night she slept without dreaming.

Peter did not talk with anybody. In his school he was one of three thousand young persons, boys and girls. For the first few weeks of life, as one of thousands, he was totally silent, studying hard and doing his best. Then he began to discover that this was not good. If he kept on being the first in classes, answering the teachers when no one else knew the answer and always prepared with his homework, his compositions in English always marked "excellent" and his problems in algebra never too hard for him, then he would not have friends. He discovered that others did not come to school for such reasons. They came to meet each other, to plan for picnics and parties, above all to plan for sports. He must learn sports if he wanted friends among them. He longed for friends, a few boys or even one to whom he could speak, to whose home he could go and whom he could take home with him to his own room, someone who liked stamps and reading and if possible someone who was not ashamed of playing the piano. He found no one like this, and so he began to consider the matter of sports. It was autumn and football was the concern. Nothing else was talked about except this one sport which he did not understand. He sat through his first football game without knowing what its purpose was. As soon as they began to play, it seemed to him, something went wrong, a whistle blew, and a man ran up and made them begin all over again. It was strange that the boys did not know how to play a game they seemed so passionately to love.

Then one day the coach asked him to come out for the game.

"You're tall and strong for your age," the man said.

"You ought to be good football material. Ever play before?"

"No, sir," Peter said. Not for any price would he reveal what had now become a shameful secret, that he had lived all his life in China. A good American should be born in his own country and stay there.

"You'll have to work at it, then," the coach said.

A gate opened before Peter. They wanted him to play football. He could learn, he could become one of the gang who was always being stopped. But he would become the best of them and then they would all be his friends.

"Thank you, sir," he said. "I would like to try."

As quickly as he could, Peter now became like the others. He stopped answering all the questions in his classes. Indeed he answered as few as possible and looked away when the teacher turned to him.

"Well, Peter?" the teacher asked when all other failed.

Sometimes he answered but sometimes he knew enough to shake his head. He was learning that one can go just so far beyond his fellows without winning their hatred instead of their love. And if he had their hatred now before they knew him well, then he would have lost their love forever, and he had to have their love. What was his country if his countrymen did not love him? He laid aside every other ambition and bent all his genius, his extraordinary understanding, the talents he did not yet know that he had, to the task of winning the affection of a handful of young brutes. Girls as yet had no meaning for him. Girls were sisters and mothers, his own or belonging to another boy.

"Peter, why do you not bring home some friends of yours?" Nadya scolded him lovingly, aware that her son went often to other houses after school but never brought boys home with him.

Young Peter blushed, unable to tell her why he could not. They would ask him the hateful questions: Why does your mother speak like a foreigner? Is she a foreigner? Is that the way Chinese talk? Is she Chinese? If she isn't Chinese, what is she? Russian? But Russians are Communists!

"Why, Peter?" Nadya persisted. She was not one to stop short of an answer.

"Oh, I dunno," he said.

"Dunno—dunno," she repeated reproachfully. "What is this language? Do not spoil beautiful English!"

"I don't know them too well yet." Thus he compromised and she let it go. She was shrewd and her guesses were as good as another's knowledge.

"Malcolm," she said that night, "I think Peter is ashamed of me. You must help him. Some trouble he is having in his school or he would bring home his friends. I make cookies, I bake a cake, but he does not bring any boys home with him."

Malcolm was instantly angry and the muscles in his face grew tense. "If Peter has the impudence to be ashamed of you——"

"No, no," she coaxed, "he loves me too much, and that is the matter. He loves me and suffers because I am not like all other mothers of all other boys. I am something different. He loves me and cannot endure it."

She calmed him and the next day he sought out his son alone after dinner. Peter was upstairs in his room, preparing his lessons. He could not keep from enjoying his books, and he often worked far beyond what was required, keeping this secret from his fellows and even from his teachers. When Malcolm came in he saw his son at the big desk he had chosen himself, the green-shaded light bent to cast its glow upon the pages of an open book.

"Peter, I want to talk to you."

"Yes, Dad?"

The tall lad stood up, as Nadya always insisted the children must when their parents came into the room. She had been taught so in China and her children must follow the ways of traditional courtesy.

"Sit down," Malcolm said. "I want to talk about your mother. She has an idea that you aren't bringing your friends home because of her."

He saw his son flush vividly and knew that Nadya as usual had hit upon the truth.

"Well, Peter?"

"It isn't that I don't want to bring fellows home, Dad."

"Then why not do so?"

"Well—they've never seen people like us, and I'm just beginning to make some friends, through football. Later when they get used to me, I thought maybe——"

He understood his son and resented his own understanding. "Your mother is beautiful and charming," he said stiffly. "I think even your friends could appreciate her."

Peter looked at his father with beseeching eyes. "They aren't used to people—to ladies—like her—being mothers." He struggled to go on. "And they don't understand about Russia at all. They'll think she's queer and maybe dangerous."

He had got it out at last. More he could not say.

Malcolm stared sternly at his son's crimson face. "I think you are ashamed of your mother."

Tears rushed to Peter's eyes. "How can you say so, Dad? I'm not ashamed—I'm proud of her—I can't bear for her to be—to be—misunderstood. It's they—it's not her. But they're the fellows I have to live with. Can't you see that?"

For an instant, briefer than thought, Malcolm wondered if they should have gone to some other country, to an older people, who would not shape themselves to so narrow a pattern. Then he thrust the thought aside. No, this was their country and they would damn well learn how to live in it. He got up and made an effort at a smile.

"I think you misjudge your friends," he told his son. "I fancy they are much better than you think. Try them! Bring a few of them home with you tomorrow and your mother will make them have such a good time that they will envy you."

They looked at each other for a long second. "Very well, Dad, I'll try."

So Peter promised, and he told himself that if it ruined him, he would make it up by football. They always wanted a good football player.

He kept his word, and the next day he brought home with him four boys from his class, an assortment of looks and sizes, but all clad in the exaggerated garments of the contemporary young, faded blue jeans and sweat shirts. When they approached the house he heard music, his mother playing the piano beautifully.

"I shall be just myself," Nadya had told her husband. "I quite see how he feels, but I am best when I am myself, and at heart surely these boys are still human beings like other boys."

So she had dressed herself carefully in a soft blue frock and had put on a handsome old Russian necklace of gold that her mother had hidden between her breasts when she fled from the ancestral home. She brushed her smooth, fair hair and coiled it low and when the boys came in she was sitting at the piano, her full skirts sweeping the floor, playing a Tschaikovsky concerto and pretending not to know that the door had opened.

"Mother," Peter said in agony. He was sure that the

other boys had no such mother as this at five o'clock in the afternoon.

She whirled about and put out her hands.

"Come in, come in——" She pulled down his head and kissed his cheek lightly. "Are these your friends, Peter? How nice!"

She smiled back at their stares.

"Harold, John, Arthur, Stover—" Peter said, not looking at them. Why did she have to kiss him? She did not always kiss him when he came home from school.

She pointed them out one by one and repeated, laughing, "Harold, John, Arthur, Stover—and the same last names? Brothers?"

"No," Peter said coldly. "Mother, we are going to do some football practice in the lower meadow."

"Without eating?" She was immensely shocked. "I cannot allow it! First some chocolate cake, if you please, and I have made ice cream myself. It is better made at home as I do it——"

She interlaced her fingers with his and drew him with her toward the kitchen. "Come, come," she persuaded them all, and the strange boys followed, staring at her, attracted, as she could see, by a mother like this, so gay, so pretty, treating her own son as if he were not a child at all but a young man, and they all became young men and wished they had at least changed their shirts, and this Nadya knew, although Peter did not.

In the kitchen she sat them down, talking and teasing.

"My Peter," she began, "he is playing football now? You must teach him American because he must teach me. I am so new here—you must all teach me! Oh, how I love this country—my country now, too! I am so happy here. Tell me how you say 'chocolate'—Peter tells me I am always saying it wrong——"

She made them each say "chocolate" slowly while she imitated them: "Chocklat—chocklit—chocklit—chocklot——"

"Peter, you didn't say it like this"—she turned to her son reproachfully. "You must teach me better or you will be ashamed of me because I am not American like all other mothers. Sad to say, but I cannot help it! Only I try."

Oh, she drove in this little barb and he felt it, but the others did not see the barb and they laughed and ate prodigiously of the rich black cake.

"Made like in old Russia," she explained, "for that was where my parents were living and I was born there and then came the Communists and we all ran away to China then, and so Peter was born in China and Lise also, and then came the Communists again to China also, and once more we ran away, always running, and this time we come home to our own country forever and we will never run again."

She explained it carelessly, gaily, and they listened, and Peter sat still as a stone, his head bent while his secret lay revealed.

"Gee, it must of been hard!"

"I sure wouldn't have liked it——"

"You won't have any trouble here, though!"

"Gosh, Peter, you never told us!"

"Gee," she said, eyebrows questioning. "Gosh—Peter, you didn't teach me this yet!"

They laughed, all except Peter, who did not lift his head.

"What is Gee?" Thus she questioned Harold.

He blushed at the touch of her pretty hand on his arm.

"Gee—well, it's just—gee. It don't have any meaning, I guess."

"And gosh is just gosh," John said smartly. They laughed and she laughed.

"Gee," Nadya said, "I am learning so much from you. Gosh—now go and play your football. That I cannot learn."

She watched them file out, daring her son as he passed. Well, Peter, her eyes declared, I am as I am, although your mother! But there was no flicker in his eyes. He does not forgive me, she thought. They walked away from her and down the brick path and she waited, half breathless. Suddenly he looked back at her. Oh, thank God! He turned his head and he lifted his hand and waved.

At the end of the year Nadya counted on her fingers the people she knew. Old Yarcy came first, for they had become friends in a guarded sort of way. He called her by no name but she overheard him speaking of her to others as She. "She don't want none of your baker's stuff," he told the wandering trucks that carried pies and cakes and bread over the countryside. "She's scared of machines," he told the salesmen for the white monuments that were the pride of other women, the washing machines and dishwashers, and freezers. To others he said, "Yeah, She's home. She don't go out much."

When she came out into the garden she waved at him and he grinned toothlessly and spat by way of greeting. Sometimes when she knelt to weed radishes or pansies, he crept up on her, his hoe over his shoulder and began talking.

"Say, my chicken house is ready to be cleaned out. I'll sell you the manure—nothin' like it for the yearth."

She sat back on her heels, and from bargaining, for she was shrewd at bargaining after all those years in Peking, they fell to talk about gardening and then she asked questions about the people who had once lived

in the house, the Mennonite women with their full
skirts and their little bonnets and the men with their
black buttoned-up coats. He gave her long, garbled
answers which she believed were half fantasy until one
day in the spring she walked down the lane to the
road and saw for herself a woman coming toward her
like a ghost, a woman all in black, the full skirt, the
long-sleeved bodice, the little bonnet framing a round,
aging face, just now startled to see her. They stopped,
each affrighted at the sight of the other.

"Do you look for someone?" Nadya asked.

The woman stood still, the wind spreading her full
skirts. "I heared of the changes in the house, and I
thout I would come and see the old place. I was born
in the house."

"Do come in," Nadya said.

"I will not come in," the woman said. "I will just
walk around by myself, if you will let me, and look at
the shrubbage."

"Please go where you will," Nadya said.

She nodded and smiled and walked away and, not
able when she reached the end of the lane to believe
what had happened, she turned and saw the heavy
figure in the black flowing skirts gazing at the changed
house. When she came home the woman was gone.

"History come alive," Malcolm said when Nadya told
him.

She did not reply. Had she or had she not really seen
the woman?

Butcher and mason, carpenter and grocer, and clerks
and shoppers, in the small county seat where they did
their shopping and with whom she mixed, people who
were gentle and friendly at the accident of touch or the
necessity of service, and ready for a moment's talk but
never going beyond the moment—these were her only

friends. No one came to see her. Once a woman stopped her on the street.

"Is it true that you have five bathrooms in your house?"

"A tiny one to each bedroom," Nadya said, smiling, "and one for guests."

"I heard so, but I couldn't hardly believe it," the woman said and, her plump face unsmiling, she went on.

Nadya could count on her fingers all such people but she had no friends. In her kitchen now was a pretty little maid, the daughter of a farmer, who had besought her for work.

"I always wanted to work for city folks," the girl said.

She was a soft and slight-voiced creature, her eyes large and brown, her English incredibly bad.

"But we shall always live here in the country," Nadya said.

"You'll be goin' to the city one of these days," the girl coaxed. "Then I'll go with you and meet a feller I know. At least we've had correspondence."

Nadya was incurably interested in humankind. "Doesn't he come to see you, my dear?" she asked in her large-hearted way.

"He can't," the girl answered. "He don't have time. He's a radio singer. But his letter tells me where he is and to come and see him when I get to the city. He'll wait for me, I guess."

Weeks later when Nadya was used to her dreaming movements about the house, the girl, Leora, pulled a letter from her blouse and showed it to Nadya proudly.

"Miz MacNeil, here's a letter I'd like for you to see. It come last week."

Nadya read it, the usual letter of a secretary hired to answer letters from lovesick adolescents, who must be teased just enough by the possibility, the hope, dream-fed, that they will see the idolized one.

"Dear Little Leora, your letter brings me the fragrance of apple blossoms, the loveliness of the woods, the wild sweetness of the hills. Keep writing to me, dear, and remember I'm singing for you. Listen for me, Leora, on Tuesday the fifteenth, when I'll be singing your favorite song, 'Somewhere a Dream Lies Sleeping.' "

"Wunnerful letter, ain't, Miz MacNeil?"

"Oh," Nadya cried aghast, "please, please, don't believe him! He has to write like this to everyone."

The large brown eyes, so shallow, so ignorant, stared at her reproachfully. "I trust him, Miss MacNeil. You don't understand."

It was enough to break the heart for a day at least, until at night she told Malcolm the story. "And what ought I now to say?" Nadya demanded. "She wishes not to know the truth."

"You have done your duty," he replied. "Besides, perhaps she needs to be in love."

But Nadya could not be detached. The next morning when Leora was cleaning the floors with the hideous machine she held up her hand and the girl stopped the noise.

"Did you want something, Miz MacNeil?"

"Leora, listen to me, my dear. I have thought so much in the night about you. Why not learn to love some nice young man hereabouts? I am sure on these beautiful farms there is a good young man, maybe even handsome, who is better for you."

Leora wrinkled her straight little nose. "One of them fellows? No, thanks! Smellin' of cows! They can't even write a decent letter. Pawin' a girl—that's all they think about."

"I am sure also they wish to marry nicely." So Nadya pleaded.

"Marry and have a lot of kids and work on a farm? No, thanks! Not me! I seen too much of it."

The machine started again and talk was impossible. Nadya shrugged her shoulders with Russian violence and went away.

When Nadya came face to face with something here in America which she did not understand she went into her flower border, a place conceived and planned with far too much of everything, so that in desperation she rushed against weeds and upheld crowding flowers. And why, she asked her universe, did the girl Leora not wish to guard herself against a man? Even as a child she herself had known that she must guard against men, for in every man there is a wilderness to be forbidden or if accepted, then contained and limited. How few men there were who did not think first of what they could get without paying a price! In fact, she had met none except Malcolm, whom therefore she had instantly loved as soon as she knew beyond doubt that he could be trusted to guard his own wildness and never to yield to it. But Malcolm was a scholar, he was an intellectual, a thinker, a man of mind as well as body, cultivated, learned, all those qualities which befit the nobly born, and how astonished she had been when she found that his father had not been titled or in any way a nobleman in the usual sense of the word, a thing not to be understood until she questioned Malcolm closely and found that in America, this country she was endeavoring so desperately to make her own, there was no nobility, and therefore no one could be nobly born in the true and ancient sense. It was to that degree a country as confused and unruly as Soviet Russia, of which she thought with fear and sorrow whenever she allowed herself to think of it at all.

The border was well weeded that day and she came in flushed and exhausted, but calm, to make the evening's dinner. Nevertheless that night when they were alone, for Lise had gone to her room to study, and Peter had said that he must go to basketball practice, Nadya attacked her husband with a gentle ferocity. He was reading something learned, a magazine upon whose cover she saw the title *The American Scholar,* words which very well described Malcolm himself, she thought. They were in the big living room, which she had almost forgotten had been other than it was, a place now made bright by many windows, and where delightful American chairs and sofas invited repose, yet where the tapestries and painted scrolls that she had brought from Peking looked not at all amiss.

She settled herself on a big hassock, her wide skirts spreading, and thus she began.

"Malcolm, please, you must stop reading!"

"Yes?" he replied but not stopping.

"I have something to say to you."

"Something you have not said before?" His face was hidden behind the magazine.

"I have not said it before as I say it now."

He let the magazine fall upon his knees. "What is it?"

Her face, vivid and charming, was subtly lit by an expression he recognized. She wanted something very doubtful, something perhaps impossible.

"You know I am happy," she proclaimed.

"My darling, I am delighted," he replied.

"At present," she amended.

"Why not forever?" he inquired.

"I can only be happy if I belong in some place," she said. "You remember, at first in Peking I was not happy.

In fact, perhaps I was never altogether happy until you told me you loved me. On that day I had someone of my own. This is necessary to my happiness in any country."

He smiled, the corners of his mouth twitching. "You still have me, my love. I am your possession, am I not?"

She was very serious, no answering smile. "Of course, Malcolm, that I know. I am also yours. But it is not the point."

"No?"

"No! Now I must have something more, something entirely American. In short, a child, born here in this house, American complete, not knowing Peking at all."

He looked at her reproachfully. "Oh, Nadya, why will you not be content? Peter and Lise are growing very American."

"Never will they be one hundred percent," she said. "I wish to have a child who has no memories except here in this house. Here he is born, here he learns to walk and to talk. The name of Peking means nothing to him, he has no imagination of it. So he is one hundred percent American."

"Why do you keep saying one hundred percent?" he demanded. "Where have you heard such a thing?"

"I read it in newspapers, books, et cetera," she said. "We should have one such child, Malcolm—altogether one hundred percent."

"One small child in a house with a lot of adults or semi-adults will be lonely."

He spoke rashly and instantly realized his mistake. For she said with a sort of ecstasy, the ecstasy into which the Russian can fall at the slightest spring of the heart. "Oh, then two, Malcolm! Two is much better—thank you!"

"Wait," he commanded. "You're rushing ahead. Lise and Peter will want to go to college. That means a lot of money. And two more? Good God, Nadya, I shall be seventy before they finish college!"

She leaned toward him, all her being in persuasion. "Two very quick, only one year between? And Peter and Lise shall help them. This is right in any case, the elder brother and sister must help the younger. The little boy is named Thomas, and the little girl, who is the younger, one year only, shall be Lucie. You see, it is all arranged."

She came to him, her skirts spreading like wings, and fell into his arms, sighing.

"Oh, Malcolm, you make me always happy!"

And he held her in his arms, loving her better than all the world besides, reflecting soberly in the midst of unutterable love, the responsibility of children. Peter and Lise had been conceived and born in another world, in other times. The old life in Peking had now the halcyon quality of dead dreams. How had he ever imagined that it would last forever? But it had lasted so long that perhaps he might be forgiven for his folly. Thousands of years had passed over the city, leaving it, century by century, more beautiful, enriched by age and the endless stream of humanity. Emperors and their courts had left their monuments behind them, palaces and pagodas, tombs of immense sculptures and stately avenues, and the dry cool air of distant deserts had embalmed the centuries and bred a race of people, tall and handsome and kingly. No wonder that men and women from the whole cultivated world had come there to live out their days! There had been no atmosphere to equal the native climate of that noble city. Freedom was its energy, freedom to be what one would, to live as one wished. He looked back on those days, when the wittiest and the wisest of a dozen nations gathered to eat and drink, to talk and make music in a Chinese courtyard, and then perhaps to go to Chinese opera and see the matchless Mei Lan-fang portray the heroines of history. And after that it was no less a pleasure to go homeward through the wide empty streets in the cool clear moonlight, meeting none except perhaps a blind singer, who, knowing neither night nor day, walked solitary, strumming his lute and singing out his heart. And the music was always gay, that he remembered, not the light gaiety of Verdi or Puccini or the strident gaiety of jazz, but the gentle laughter that is the final expression of a wisdom too great to be unkind.

In that world, seemingly so safe, he had begotten his son and his daughter, believing them fortunate to be born into it. And why, he asked himself, holding his beloved in his arms, did he fear now to beget other children? Surely these quiet hills and old farmsteads were enduring, more enduring perhaps than the palaces of Peking. The plain people among whom he had chosen to make his present home were the eternal ones, the unchanging of any land. What was there to fear in his own country? Nothing, perhaps, except the uncertainty of his own knowledge of it! He did not know how his country might have changed in the years since his own youth, the years in which he had been away. These months since the house had been finished he had been living not here but in history, and when he went into his study in the morning he returned to the other land. He ought in fairness to the unborn to know much more than he did about his own country.

"What would you say if I ask you to wait until I finish my book?"

He put this question to Nadya and she answered strongly, as he knew she would.

"I say no, Malcolm! I cannot wait upon a book to begin my new living."

He sighed, yet was not a little stirred. He was a man

so virile that in him passion was more than appetite. He loved this woman whole, and not only all his love was hers, but all his passion. That night, when he felt her body cling to his, he yielded, at first reluctant, until the barriers broke in consummation, complete and irrevocable.

Summer lay fallow upon the land and Nadya at the window looked up to gaze dreamily over the landscape. No other house was in sight, not in summer when the trees were in full leaf. In winter when trees were bare one could see at the end of the road over the bridge the rooflines of the village beyond, a handful of houses, with barns and garages. She was happy, not, she knew, with permanent happiness, for one could not enjoy forever the isolation of pregnancy, the relief from responsibility for the world around. Nine months of irresponsibility and after that a year of babyhood, at most two, and then the small creature would be running about alone and she would have to begin to think again. But could she not subdue herself to the small creature and learn as he grew? To come to a new country, one in whose history she had no share whatever, whose language she had acquired as foreign, and yet to which she was attached by the deepest emotion of her life, her love for her American husband, this was a strange and dividing experience. For America itself was more foreign to her than any other country she had yet known. Her noble Russian parents had reared her in the atmosphere of exalted freedom, a personal freedom, where nothing was hidden from anyone, where laughter and tears and anger and tenderness came as they would. Tenderness was the touchstone of the refugees who had fled from their country when communism broke. Never to wound one another, never to seem unloving or unkind, these were the necessary compensations for being homeless and destitute. If those in trouble do not love each other, then what is there left in life? And the Chinese in their own way had the same quality. "Face," it was called in their language, and yet what was it but tenderness? The human face is all that distinguishes one human creature from another. Bodies, tall or short, fat or thin, are much the same, but no face is like any other, and therefore consider the face of each one, and cause no shadow of sorrow upon it.

To cause sorrow to another person, individual and particular, that, Nadya believed, was sin. The massive sorrows of life cannot be avoided. Disaster and catastrophe fall alike upon the just and the unjust and can be endured, for these do not break the heart. It is the little knives that cut, the slighting word, the lack of love. She believed in love, the large and enveloping love that accepts all human beings as they are. Love was as essential to her as air and she examined unconsciously every creature to discover whether there was love in that heart. Even the animals that had gradually come to the house, the cocker spaniel puppies Malcolm had bought for the children, the copper brown male for Peter, the small brown female for Lise, Nadya had not accepted into the family until she had discovered for herself that they were gentle. And she had refused to shelter a tomcat because she saw him kill the kittens he had bred into the gray barn cat. Yet she knew from bitter life experience that not every creature is good and loving. There are those who from birth are cruel and bloodthirsty, unable to love. She pondered upon them and one day she questioned Malcolm. Thinking of the savage tomcat had made her think of Chen Chi-tang.

"My dear," she asked, "do you think that a man like

Chen Chi-tang could have been good if he had received much kindness from childhood?"

Chen Chi-tang had been a member of the secret police in Peking, a man so ruthless that he was called the Black Devil by the people on the streets.

Malcolm, arriving at this moment with an armful of wood for the fireplace, put his mind at once to work. Long ago he had taught himself not to be irritated at the seeming irrelevance of Nadya's questions, annoying though it was to one of his orderly nature to be assailed with a question requiring consideration before it could be answered. He had learned, nevertheless, that did he untangle the skeins of Nadya's thought, he would discover relevance.

"Who knows?" he now replied. He dusted from his hands and his garments the fragrant bits of dry wood. In his spare time he was cleaning out the choked orchard and finding the treasure of old apple trees, the Baldwin and the Northern Spy, the Maiden's Blush and the June Sweet.

"I am asking only what you think," Nadya said with emphasis.

She was crocheting a small sacque in the intricate shell stitch she had learned from her mother in Manchuria. There a bit of sheep's wool had been treasure and during wars they had been reduced to using camel's wool, still stinking of the beast. To soak the clammy stuff in carbolic acid solution was the only way to cleanse it of camel reek, and then it was to reek of carbolic. She gloated now over the richness of the soft fine wools, preshrunk and fast-hued. She admired extravagantly the genius of America, where everything was done well. How to become part of all this genius?

Malcolm postponed his return to work, although he was now reaching the crucial point in his study of the Chinese revolution, that moment when the union between peasant and intellectual in Chinese history was in modern times to result in the final triumph of communism. What did it prove? That neither peasant nor intellectual could succeed without each other in a revolution? Yet in the end the peasant killed the intellectual!

He retrieved his mind from its own question and sat down to answer Nadya. "You are asking whether some people are born to be evil. I think not. I cannot tell where the hardening begins but not, I believe, before birth."

Nadya's mobile face quivered and smiled. "Thank you, my dear, then I am not frightened. For if what you say is true there is hope for us all. It is hopelessness only that I fear."

"That is not to say that you can reform people already hopeless," Malcolm reminded her.

"Oh no," she agreed. "I am not a child, Malcolm. There are some who can only be avoided until death. I wish not to remember them."

Chen Chi-tang was one of them, he knew—that cruel man who had killed all who opposed him! He was a peasant and the son of a peasant.

He leaned forward, elbows on his knees and hands hanging clasped. "Nadya, why did they kill the intellectuals in Russia?"

He saw sadness settle over her face. Small muscles under that smooth white skin drooped and tightened. She let her hands drop in her lap and the soft pile of rosy wool fell over them.

"It is such a hard question." She lifted her eyes and fixed them by chance on his hands, big thin hands, working hands, she thought them, and yet the hands of an intellectual, very American hands, expressing genius.

"In Russia," she said, "we had everything divided very clear—too clear. Serfs upon our land I remember so well, and never could they be anything but serfs. And my family, we never thought ourselves anything but intellectuals, except we were noble also. But somehow all the intellectuals were noble, big noble and small noble. We were big noble, very near the Czar. Yet I did understand also how the serfs could feel. I remember our carriage rolling in the springtime from Moscow to our land, where always we spent the summer, and the little serf children ran after, and my mother, meaning kindness, threw out candies she had bought especially for the purpose and the candies fell into the mud and the children, screaming with joy, picked them up with mud, too, and ate them so happily. And afterwards I remember reading when I was growing up in Harbin some Communist paper from Moscow and a young student in chemistry, a girl from our land but now graduating from the university, blamed my parents so much because my mother threw the candies and they fell in the mud, and the serf children had to eat mud with the candies. She was one of those children! This she spoke as the great cruelty of her childhood, that with the candies she had also to eat mud.

"It would have been better, naturally, if my mother had thrown no candies at all. Yet, I asked myself, why didn't my mother, so beautifully educated, know how it was to a child to eat the mud with the candies? One day I even asked her, 'Mamá, why didn't you stop the carriage and give the candies clean to the serf children?' She said, 'Nadya, you cannot remember, but if I did it those children would climb all over the carriage and demand so much and maybe give an illness to my own children. So I could only throw the candies as I passed, poor little souls.' She was really sorry, and yet she could see no way. And I think that the girl, remembering how tasted the mud in her mouth, would have killed my mother in the revolution if she could. But my father, understanding the danger, had already taken us away. Such little things, all making together a terrible revolution!"

This was typical Nadya talk. She could compress into one incident, one example, the whole truth of an epoch.

"And so the intellectuals ran away," he said.

She agreed, her eyes suddenly very clear and blue, lifting to his face. "We ran away because we didn't think soon enough what else to do. And also it was no use to Russia that we be killed, although many were killed."

She paused, thinking hard and concentrated thoughts.

"And Malcolm, old Yarcy, he is like a serf, but he is free, and there are others here like the serfs, but all are free. Everything is moving here, nothing is tied to land or tree or house and I should like to know how it got in this way, freely moving, so that a serf kind of man can still feel himself so free and his children can go to school, and the intellectual needs not to run away because if he so wishes he can become a serf again. This is how America is free, I think."

He was not ready yet to think about his own country. He had first to rid himself of China. There peasant and scholar, in combination, had defeated every tyrant until the empire fell. It had fallen finally because a young peasant by chance had become also a scholar, the leader in his moment of vast, slow revolution. A first-generation scholar is a dangerous man. He is always too practical. He dreams but he wants to make his dreams come true and this makes him the most dangerous man in the world.

Malcolm got up and went back to his quiet room, anxious to impale his thought before it escaped him. Nadya watched him with loving eyes, understanding because she loved him, and when he was gone she took up the rosy wool again to make a garment for their child.

"Mamá," Lise said, "Let us go to church now like other Americans."

Nadya looked up from the rosebed. Wherever she had lived she had always planted roses. In Peking the inner wall had been lined with a deep row of Shantung roses, small yellow flowers that bloomed solidly gold in the early summer. She had found the same roses in an American nurseryman's catalogue and she had planted them now against the stone foundation of the barn, and she had made two wide beds across the far end of the lawn for her tea roses. Now she looked up at her daughter.

"Today you want to go?"

She tried not to be astonished. Church, yes, it was possible, but the Sundays were precious, and to spend the morning in a building when one could work outdoors, the sky the roof, was this not regrettable?

"I don't care, Mamá, when we begin, but we should begin," Lise said. "All nice people go to church."

Nadya laughed. "Yet you know only the nice people hereabouts and not in all America!"

"In my two aunties' houses, they go," Lise insisted. When she was speaking with her mother her English reverted to that which she had first learned. She had no accent, but her words were staccato and foreign. When she talked to her schoolmates her language was entirely different. Nadya had often heard this child with schoolmates, and then Lise's voice was almost like those of the other Americans. Nasal, clear, and loud, the children talked together.

Nadya put down her trowel with inward reluctance and outward cheerfulness. "Let us go," she said. "If your father and Peter are unwilling, you and I will go. And we will go every Sunday, my darling, so long as you wish."

Somewhat to her surprise, Malcolm was willing, and Peter, also. Each was in his own room, apparently happy, and Peter was even making a fishing rod. Nevertheless, he rose willingly enough at Lise's invitation. In less than half an hour, when the church bells were ringing, they went driving up the road toward the nearest town where around a solid small red brick church the crowd was gathering to go in. A pretty sight, Nadya thought, the young women's dresses light-colored, rose and white and blue, the older women in gray and brown and black, and the men in their solemn colors except for the bright ties of the young men, and what bright ties!

It was pleasantly strange to walk quietly into the church and see the sunshine slanting through the tall windows, the rays converging upon the central aisle, and the people walking in in a silver mist of light. Beautiful, Nadya thought, and when the music began softly from the hidden organ emotion stirred her heart, soft and sad. She wished to pray, although she had nothing for which to pray now, happy as she was, but prayer could also be thanksgiving and she knelt in her pew for an instant, in the way she remembered her mother had done in the Greek Catholic church in Harbin. Suddenly she felt a touch on her shoulder. It was Lise again, with a whisper, agitated and sharp.

"Mamá, nobody is kneeling!"

Nadya sat down, but she could not forebear a reproach. "Lise, my dear, each person prays as he likes best, surely."

"Mamá, people are staring at you," Lise said.

Nadya glanced about and saw that people were indeed staring at them, curiously, not unkindly, merely perhaps surprised that this new family had come to church at last.

She looked straight ahead of her then while the music played and after a time she stole a look at Malcolm. He was lost in thought, unconscious of her, and she took the opportunity to admire again his fine profile, his noble head, his broad shoulders. In the light she saw gray hairs glistening on his temples and in his dark hair. My beautiful, she thought, are you really getting old? But no, he was as young as ever, as passionate a lover, as keen a mind. Beyond him sat Peter, so like his father except that she had bestowed upon her son her blondness, and the slightly sharpened lines of brow and nose and chin. The boy's head was lifted and his eyes were fixed on the gold cross in the chancel of the church. Somewhere an electric light was fastened high under the beams so that an intense brilliance shone upon that cross.

The music changed and softened and the minister, Owen Hastings, came from a door in the chancel, clothed in a long black robe like a priest. He moved to the pulpit, so young a man but with dignity, and there he lifted his hands and the congregation rose while he blessed them with prayer.

Nadya listened closely to the words: "Grant, Father God, that in this hour we spend in worship our hearts may be subdued to learn Thy Will."

A good prayer, she thought, a humble prayer, and she repeated it, whispering it softly.

"Mamá!" Lise's rebuking voice came again in her ear. "Be quiet, please!"

"I am only praying," she whispered to Lise with indignation.

"Mamá, please!" Lise begged.

Malcolm turned his head. "What's the matter?" he asked, also in a whisper.

Now it was Peter's turn. He did not speak but he put his finger on his lip.

Nadya shook her head and quiet fell again. A hymn was to be sung. Malcolm took a book from a narrow shelf and found the place and he shared his book with Nadya. The choir burst into song and the congregation joined with them slowly and carefully. Nadya listened for a moment, not daring to sing aloud, because of Lise. Then she heard Lise's voice, and was this not permission? She lifted her head and let out her voice loud and clear, enjoying the music she herself made. Only when the hymn was nearly ended did she happen to notice that now Lise was not singing at all.

She sat down again with the others and, finding Malcolm's hand, she clasped it and sat happily with him. It was pleasant, this church-going, and Lise was right. The minister read Scripture, beautiful words which she heard for the first time. "Let not your hearts be troubled," he read, and that was pleasant. The heart was so easily troubled. "Ye believe in God, believe also in me." In me? Did he mean himself, this young man? Well, perhaps he knew something, too. She sat relaxed and ready to receive more music and another hymn, another reading, and then the congregation seemed to settle itself.

"What comes now?" she whispered to Malcolm.

"The sermon," he whispered back.

She nodded and gazed steadfastly at the tall young figure ascending a higher pulpit at the other end of the chancel.

He read again. "He that is not for me is against me——"

She frowned unconsciously, trying to drain the meaning from these words. Alone, there could be any meaning, she thought, and she must wait to hear them explained. Then somehow her mind slipped out of the church. She began to think of her roses. She had two fine bushes of a rose named Peace. A peace rose, she thought, how beautiful an imagination! It had not yet bloomed but she had read the catalogue description, a creamy rose, touched with gold and pink, a very queen of a rose. She thought of her garden and then inevitably of her dear house, her own house, which no one could ever take from her, nor from which she could ever be driven. There were no mobs here in America, no angry people surging into houses to rob and destroy. Think how it had been in Russia, which she herself could not remember, but which she had heard her parents describe, poor Papá, his beard quivering because he was trying not to weep, and Mamá sobbing aloud, her handkerchief to her eyes. The wonderful big house where all her ancestors had been born, where they had lived and died, was finally destroyed by the serfs who had helped to build it. Yes, they had utterly destroyed that to which they had belonged, and Papá and Mamá had escaped like beggars, walking the dreary miles, hundreds of miles, to Manchuria and Harbin. She could barely remember the wretched house in Harbin, but from that they had been driven, too, when the Japanese took the city and then the dreadful march had begun again to Peking. And Peking had seemed so safe, she had grown up there, she had been educated, mostly by Papá and Mamá, and then she had begun the endless teaching of languages in a Chinese university—French, English, Russian, German, all the languages Papá and Mamá had taught her—until she had met Malcolm. From the moment when she had looked up into his dark kind eyes, she had lived in heaven. Yes, actually, such love was heaven, and now he had brought her here to his own beautiful country. She lifted his hand impulsively and kissed it. He was somewhat startled but he smiled. It remained for Peter and Lise to reproach her with their accusing eyes, their faces blushing because she was their mother.

She would have been angry except that at this moment she heard the minister say in his stern young voice, "Today the whole world is divided into two, Christian and Communist. Those who are not Christian are Communist. There can be no compromise."

Oh, she said under her breath. She bit her lip. She was amazed. How could he say such a thing?

"Not true!" she whispered to Malcolm.

He agreed by the slightest inclination of his head but otherwise he remained immovable. She could not listen any more. For if a man said such a thing, he was a liar or he was ignorant, and in either case he was not to be believed. It was too bad, this nice young Owen Hastings did not know what he said. Indeed she did fear Communists, and who had suffered from them more than she? Yet surely one must know that most of the people in the world, nevertheless, were not Communist, nor were they Christian. Consider, please, she silently besought the young minister, how there are also all the Hindus, the Muslims, the Buddhists, and in China the many who were still Taoist and Confucian! Also, she suggested silently, are there not many who cannot believe, but who wait nevertheless with reverent hearts to discover the truth!

She glanced at her children, first at Lise and then at Peter. Surely they must not be taught to narrow their hearts and minds. To divide all peoples into two, forcing them under one banner or the other, refusing them freedom! No, no, it is not good, she thought.

But she could not speak. That was denied her. Here in the church one must listen but not answer. Her heart, unrepressed by habit, instantly filled with resentment. And why was it allowed to this young priest to speak unreproved? Why did he not read from the Scriptures and let God do the speaking?

In this midst of the resentment he suddenly finished what he had to say and the people rose to sing a parting hymn and receive the benediction. The organ played a joyful theme, and the people left the seats and thronged into the aisles. At the door by some miraculous speed Owen Hastings stood in his robes, a bright smile on his face, his hand outstretched.

"I am so glad to see the MacNeil family." His hands reached out to them all at once. "Come again, won't you? Lise, Peter, bring your parents any Sunday. A child shall lead them!"

Nadya could not but speak. She was of a terrible honesty and she could not merely smile and pass. "But you must know," she said earnestly, "you are quite wrong when you say the world is divided only into Christians and Communists. Most peoples are neither one nor the other. They have their own ways of thinking."

"Mamá!" Lise cried. "People are waiting behind you."

The minister looked shocked. Nevertheless, he only said in an amiable voice, "Let's talk about that sometime, Mrs. MacNeil."

"Mamá," Lise cried again, all but sobbing now.

So she was compelled to go on and no one said anything until they were in the car again and alone.

"Lise," Nadya said in a sad voice, "I cannot help it, I must speak. I know what I have suffered, but I think the minister knows nothing of such matters. He really should think."

"Don't take him seriously, Nadya," Malcolm said in a comfortable voice.

"But the people were listening to him, so quiet, so receiving!"

"Mamá," Peter said, "perhaps it is you who are wrong."

"Anyway," Lise put in, "it is not proper to say such things to the minister. You should shake his hand and go on. Everybody was staring at you."

They were surprised to see their father, usually so quiet and gentle, lose his temper violently and suddenly. He slowed the car and glared at them in the back seat. "Your mother is right," he said firmly. "And I will not have her changed."

Nadya suddenly began to weep. "Oh Malcolm, thank you, my dear! I thank you so much! But we must remember they are our children. We must love them always."

At this, Lise also began to cry, frightened by what she had done, and then Peter, struggling, felt the tears hot against his own eyelids. It was horrible, he did not want to cry. American boys never cried, he had not seen one do so. But when his mother wept, his own mother who was all love and goodness, and only ignorant because she was not yet American, he could not hold back. "Mamá," he said in a broken voice, "of course we love you."

"Oh, we do love you," Lise echoed, sobbing, "only——"

Malcolm waited, accustomed to his family. At last he spoke. "Now, we all understand one another. We love each other, and we must be patient with each other. And at the moment we are all hungry. We had better go home and get some food."

Nadya wiped her eyes, her voice brightly tender. "I love you all, my darlings!"

Peter and Lise stood watching old Yarcy. It was a Friday afternoon, hot and sunny, and his cheek was swelled to capacity. In the folds of his wrinkles the week's dirt lay deep, so that his face seemed to be etched in dark lines. He wore a pair of ragged leather gloves and in one hand he held a large squirming gray rat, and in the other a paint brush which he dipped into a small can of tar. Then he began to paint the frantic animal methodically.

"There ain't no better way to get rid of big rats," he was saying. "Cats are afeared of 'em. Rats know it and they take the place. Pison they enjoy to eat. But you tar one 'em like thisyere, and then let him go. He runs back to his kind, not knowing he ain't really a rat no more. He don't know it until all the other rats see him and smell him. They don't reckonize him, see? They drawr away. Who the devil are you? That's what they say in their rat talk."

They were much too old for this sort of thing, Peter and Lise, but they were fascinated. "And what does he say then?" Lise asked.

"He sticks out his whiskers," old Yarcy continued, "and he says, don't ye know me, fellers? Why, I'm old Gray Beard. Go on, they says, your whiskers ain't even gray. They're black and sticky. What, he yells. Why, look at yerself, they tells him. So he looks in the pond or a puddle and he sees he ain't what he thought he was. He ain't himself; they're right. And they leave him on the spot, because they don't want nothin' more to do with him. And he's left alone and he hasn't no heart to foller. He knows it's no use."

"What does he do then?" Lise asked.

"He lays down and dies," old Yarcy said solemnly. He painted the rat's whiskers carefully. The creature had given up and lay panting in his hand.

"There," Yarcy said, "that's the job." He released the rat and it ran for a hole in the wall. Yarcy ground tar off his hands with dry earth and grinned at them.

"Poor thing," Lise said.

"Ain't no use callin' a rat a pore thing," Yarcy said. "They has to be killed and that's all there is to it. It's rats or men, one or the other."

He picked up the hoe which he had dropped when Nadya called him and ambled off toward the patch, as he called the vegetable garden.

"Still I feel sorry," Lise said.

"I don't," Peter said. "The fellows kill rats in the old quarry every Sunday and I'm going to buy me a twenty-two and go shooting with them."

They sat down on the low stone wall around the terrace. Lise said, "I know you have to be American, Peter, but I don't like you so well as I did before."

"That is not because I am an American," he replied. "It is because we are beginning to grow up and you are reaching the age when you don't like any boys. I read about this in a book in the library. It is the age when boys gang with boys and girls with girls."

Lise did not answer. Her brother had always the advantage of her, because he continued to read secretly and incessantly, accumulating knowledge, while outwardly he pretended as a healthy American boy to scorn books. She was not able to live this double life. She was wholeheartedly a girl with other girls. Sitting there on the stone wall, the landscape spreading about her, gorgeous with summer green, she felt a strange wrenching homesickness for the compound in Peking. Behind those walls of life had seemed always safe. Here there were no walls and the fields went rolling on over the horizons. There was no protection, not unless one went into the house and closed the doors. But her mother did not like the doors shut. Windows and doors must be open to sunshine and wind. Even in winter the shades were high and the landscape was there in the room with them. There was too much of it; she yearned to square away just a little piece of it and make it all her own.

"So long," Peter said indifferently. "I'm going down to the woods."

"You might ask me to go with you," she shrieked after him.

"Come if you want to," he shouted back over his shoulder.

"But do you want me?" she cried.

He did not hear her, or if he heard he did not answer. He kept on walking down the hill to the woods.

In his small old room Malcolm wove the web of his book as the months passed by. He was more happy than he had ever been in his life, and he accused himself in his private thoughts. Undoubtedly he was writing too long a book, he was putting too much into it, and could this be because he did not want to finish it? With the book as his work, and indeed his duty, he was excused, or he excused himself, from the active life that he must begin when it was finished. He had not, for example, once written either to Corinne or to Susanna since he had visited those two houses. This surely was scarcely the behavior of a brother. And Nadya was bearing almost alone the tasks of the house and the children, sparing him, as he well knew, the many interruptions of the days when school was over and the two children always at home. He was not even sure that Lise and Peter were happy, separated by vacation from their schoolmates. Yet none of these delinquencies on his part could prevent him from opening the door of this room each morning and staying at his desk until he heard the big bell under the eaves of the kitchen ring for a meal. Peter cut the grass and fed the chickens Nadya had somehow accumulated and it was upon Peter that she called when the machines she so hated and yet which she must use in lieu of servants failed to work. She was teaching Lise to clean house and make beds and help with the mending. She was giving them both piano lessons, too, and he was scarcely aware of it except that the sound of Tschaikovsky's music floating through the open windows added to the pleasant atmosphere in his little room.

On this morning in August, he worked with more than his usual zeal. He was over the peak, he had surmounted the discouragement inevitable to growing complexity of thought, and now he had only to sort out his main arguments and draw them firmly to conclusion. He sat down before his desk and took up his pen.

"For many centuries," he wrote, "the educated men of China have not accepted as rational belief the dogmas of the supernatural in religion. What has been a precious creed to the West, a faith by which to live, has been for the intelligent Chinese mere superstition, designed to keep the ignorant in a state of submission. If Heaven, as the Chinese call it, or God, as we call it, can be blamed for catastrophe, then religion had its uses only for the earthly ruler who is negligent of the welfare of the people. But no Chinese of any pretension to literacy would accept such superstitions for his own faith. He was interested in a heaven here on earth, a practical benefit to his daily living. There is nothing strange or alien therefore, to him, in the godlessness of the Communist creed. Nor does he fear its tyranny, which to him seems much the same as the old Confucian orthodoxy, except that the new orthodoxy looks to the future, whereas Confucianism drew from the past. And he is accustomed to an orthodoxy which declares itself supreme and therefore always right, as Confucianism did so declare. The danger to us, who cannot accept such a creed, is that Mao Tse-tung's communism fulfills the Chinese tradition. Heaven, he declares, is to be upon this earth, and is to be attained not by vague and unseen gods but by the efforts of men. Mao maintains that he and his party provide the program for such effort. Herein hides our true dilemma. It is spiritual as well as practical; it captivates the idealism of the Asian peasant and the intellectual alike. Therefore with spiritual as well as practical weapons we must do combat."

He put down his pen and sighed. He was writing words, each freighted with terrible meaning, but would anyone understand? He longed for a sign, as prophets have always longed for a sign, and did not know where to seek for it. To know the truth could be a fearful burden unless the knowledge was shared. Was there no one except himself who could grasp the urgency of the danger of not understanding this crisis of human history? Men saw it partially and responded in the partial ways of a vaster army, a combing of secret spies, but this was not the true attack. And the book, upon which he had spent all these months, who would read it, even if he could get it published? It was not a story, a swashbuckling tale of the past, there was no love interest. He had told the stark events which he had seen come to pass over a quarter of a century in China, and he had proved what he believed, that the past years were only an introduction to the present.

He got up restlessly and began to pace the floor. From the huge dark fireplace to the opposite end of the room were fifteen long steps. He paced them off and turned and paced them back again. If he could get to people direct and face to face, talk to them, tell them, teach them the history they did not know, the history of the white man on the other side of the world, and from that history show them the probabilities of the white man and his future, not a hopeless future, oh not at all, unless the present chance were lost. He would show them the future as an opportunity greater than any ever given before to any of the human race. The old leadership could prevail again, but only now if the weapons were spiritual as well as material. Thinking of what he would say, imagining before him audiences of people, their faces upturned to hear him, he suddenly made up his mind. Yes, that he would do. He was no preacher, and he would not preach. He would simply reveal the past and from it explain the future—the two futures, one inevitable if the present course went on, and the other possible, if——

He opened the door of his little room and went to search for his Nadya. She was difficult to find, bustling somewhere about the house, singing from some upper floor, and he had finally to stand on the stair and shout aloud.

"Nadya, come here!"

He heard her running footsteps down the stairs from the third floor and cried out again. "Be careful—you mustn't trip!"

"No, no," she said in her singing voice. "I am used now to these old stairs——"

She arrived at the top of the stairs where he stood looking up. She was slightly out of breath and her cheeks were pink.

"What has happened, Malcolm?" she exclaimed. She kept on coming down the stairs and he caught her in his arms at the bottom, a thickened figure, her slenderness gone and even the delicacy of her face dimmed, and yet she was beautiful with vitality. She was thoroughly and unashamedly pregnant, she enjoyed being so, and he was compelled to laugh at her, all breathless and panting as she was.

"Nadya, sit down," he said. They sat down on the bottom step, his arm about her shoulder. "What would you say if after our child is born and I have finished my book that I go on a lecture tour?"

She knitted her mobile brows at him.

"Saying what, Malcolm?" she inquired.

He outlined to her quickly in large words just what he would say.

"It is in my book," he said finally, "but will my people read a book, Nadya? I fear not. But if I go about speaking, then perhaps they will want the book. You see, they need to discover that they do not know what must be known if people like us are not to be driven from one country to another. Your family driven from Russia, and now our family driven from China, and from here there is nowhere for us to go, Nadya."

She looked at him, frightened. "Oh, do so then, Malcolm! Speak all that you know. Tell them how it happens."

"I don't mean to frighten you, Nadya," he said in his reasonable way. "Actually there is no danger for us here, not now, but so we thought in Peking, only a few years ago."

"And so my parents thought in Russia," she said sadly. "They could not believe it, not until the very night when they had to flee. Oh, yes, you must go, Malcolm!"

It was one of her virtues that her mind was so quick, her imagination so ready, that she could see exactly what he meant, and that she had not a thought of herself. She did not say to him, "And how shall I manage when you are gone?" Instead she surprised him after a moment by asking for a strange thing.

"Malcolm, while you are gone, I should like to make here a real farm."

"A farm?" he repeated stupidly.

"Some cows and pigs, please," she urged, "to keep me very busy. And the milk is so good for the children.

I want them to have the fresh milk, not in bottles, not half boiled as we buy it now, but pure from the cows. While you are gone I shall make such a farm and take care of the children, and then I shall not be lonely."

"But you will need to have a farmer to help you," he exclaimed.

"Yes, a young man, perhaps, and he can live in the little house."

There was such a little house, below the hill, a small two-story structure of stone, two rooms and a kitchen. It was quite possible to make it livable. Nevertheless he protested.

"But, Nadya, you are no farmer, and you know nothing about it!"

"I come from the land, though, Malcolm," she answered in a serious tone. "My family lived always on the land. We belong to it as much as the serfs did. That is something the Communists never could think, yet it was true. The land was ours, but we belonged to the land, also. In his own way my grandfather and my father and all the men before them spent themselves on the land. If they did not pull the plow actually as the serfs did, yet the burden of making the land produce did weigh upon them as it never did upon the serf. And my father said he was never again so happy after he left his land. I like a farm, please, Malcolm!"

It was the old land hunger in her, inherited from generations of landowning ancestors, an emotion as valid, indeed, as any peasant's.

"Well, my dear"—he got up from the step and stood with his hands in his pockets looking down on her—"I shan't forbid it. Only please remember that I am not yet earning any money."

Nadya looked shocked. "Certainly I shall not spend more money than I can save," she declared. The light of creation shone in her eyes. A farm! She must begin to plan. Peter could help very much, too. It would be good for him. He could ride a tractor and plow the land. A tractor she must have, of course. All American farms had tractors.

Malcolm stooped to kiss her. "I must get back to my work," he said and left her.

A farm might be a very good thing. It would deepen their roots. There was plenty of land in the eighty acres he had bought, much of it fertile, or it could be brought back to fertility. He must warn Nadya against too much expansion, too many cows, for example. Her nature always led her toward expansion. Yet she was shrewd, she would manage. And it would be good for the children to be compelled to help her and he himself would help when once his task was done.

He sat down again to his book in deep content. He had made a decision, too quickly perhaps, but great decisions were usually so made. Actually he never decided quickly. A final determination was always the result, crystallized as swiftly as one pleased, but out of years before. So disasters fell also, never solitary and unexplained as people imagined, but only after previous action, long continued in hidden places. Even an earthquake, sudden as it seemed to those whom it engulfed, was the result of aeons before, aeons of shifting movement in the hidden earth.

The American child, Thomas MacNeil, was born on a fine bright day in April, an Aries child. Nadya had refused to go to the hospital and in this was encouraged by Dr. Brenner, the white-haired doctor, who fulfilled in all ways the stereotype of a country doctor, except that after the winter, when Spring returned, he went to Florida for three weeks and indulged himself in wild and strange activities. Nobody knew exactly what these were, but old Yarcy told Nadya that the doctor had a fancy girl there and Mrs. Brenner knew and didn't say nawthin.

"For a fact," Yarcy said, "what kin a woman say? She kin take it or leave it, and old Doc is a savin' man, well heeled, they say. He's respec'ful to Miz Brenner—that's his trick. A woman can stand a lot from a man, they say, if he's respec'ful. I dunno."

He spat, and went off to potter. Nadya gazed after him thoughtfully. Yarcy had grown as faithful as the dogs, though almost as useless. But she could not imagine being without him now. He explained to her something of America.

On this spring morning in the midst of brilliant sunshine, she felt the surge of sudden pain, and she hurried to find Malcolm, both hands clutching her waist. She never had her babies decently in the darkness.

"Malcolm!" she cried, appearing at his door, her hair blowing about her flushed face, and her ruffled apron fluttering. "Here I am taken in the midst of my morning's work! How is it I can never have my babies in nice darkness?"

He dropped his pen. "I will call Dr. Brenner."

"Yes, please, Malcolm!"

"Lean on me, my love."

He led her upstairs to her room, avoiding the eyes of Leora, cleaning on the stairs, and then he helped her to undress and put on one of the soft and voluminous Russian nightgowns which she had never given up wearing. In bed she smiled at him faintly.

"Such a thing! Do you remember how Peter broke his waters on a Sunday when we had gone to church because it was Easter? And Lise, too, she began to be born when we were having our luncheon in the courtyard in Peking that hot day—oh, so hot, in August! Do you remember?"

"Of course, my darling."

And how could he forget? She had laughed at herself in the midst of pain. "Such a mischief!" she had cried.

"This time you are in your own house," he went on, "and now I must call Dr. Brenner."

By the time the doctor came with his shapeless black leather bag, everything was ready, pots of hot water boiling on the stove and Leora waiting to fetch and carry. She was disapproving, her gravity suggesting that these foreigners from China were too queer for her. Mr. MacNeil, for instance, staying in the room while his wife was having the baby! What was that but indecent?

It would not have occurred to Nadya not to have her husband beside her. She had clung to his hands when Peter was born and had turned to him in triumph when Lise came forth so easily that she had scarcely an hour of pain.

"I wish every woman had 'em like this," Dr. Brenner said heartily. He had once been a very fat man and had lost flesh so that now his skin was closely wrinkled. Since he had just come back from Florida he was sunburned and his blue eyes were startling.

"My wife does everything well," Malcolm said.

Nadya laughed restlessly, her eyes bright with pain. It was not too bad, but this was going to be a big baby. She had eaten much good food, for she did not believe in starving unborn babies just to have an easy time herself.

"Quick," she said, breathless, "my little American is coming! He is here—he is here!"

Dr. Brenner stooped in haste and delivered Thomas MacNeil. He was a large child, and he opened his eyes astonished at the new world, his round face quivering.

"Congratulations," Dr. Brenner said. "I didn't even have time to give your mother a dash of chloroform."

"Not needed," Nadya said, panting, "never needed by me! My mother—told me, 'Nadya, no chloroform—God doesn't mean it——'"

"It's all right for *you* to believe that," Dr. Brenner retorted. "Take your son, MacNeil, and clean him up."

Young Thomas was now bellowing healthfully and Malcolm wrapped him in a soft small blanket and sat down with him and began the pleasant task. He had warmed olive oil and taking a wad of sterile cotton he rubbed his son with the benign fluid. This was Nadya's way and she watched him, her languid eyes tender and happy.

"So big, isn't he?" she murmured. "So American!"

"He'll be a football player," Dr. Brenner agreed.

Another doctor would have brought a nurse along but he didn't like nurses except in hospitals where a doctor had to have them because they ran things. He liked to see his patients through by himself, and he knew then that things were really right. Nurses covered up with all their fixings. Besides, this patient was a pleasure. She was healthy and clean and she functioned as a good animal should and without fuss. Most women made such a fuss. And the man, sitting there cleaning his baby, he'd never seen such a sight before, but it was nice.

"You're very handy," he said to Malcolm. "Where'd you learn it?"

Nadya boasted from her bed, though she was growing drowsy. "It is natural for him. Also I like it. Strangers should not be the first to care for one's child."

She drifted off with this and Malcolm, his task carefully done, wrapped his son in a clean blanket and laid him in the crib nearby. Nadya insisted that her baby must always stay near her. "So that I may see what I have! Also, I tell you, the baby knows."

The two men, husband and doctor, moved silently

about the room, putting it in order, taking away what was soiled, washing up. They tiptoed to the door and went out. Mother and child were deep in sleep and the two men smiled at each other. Doctor Brenner took out his watch. "Exactly two hours and seventeen minutes—good work! You are a fortunate man. Is she French?"

"Russian," Malcolm said distinctly, "White Russian. Her family escaped from the Bolshevists."

Doctor Brenner was indifferent. All that stuff had happened on the other side of the world somewhere, and he never read a paper except the local county sheet. When he went to Florida he read no newspapers at all. That's why he kept Isabel down there. She could make a man forget anything.

"Well, I don't know much about foreigners," he said, "but you've got a good healthy woman. Are they all like that?"

"Nobody is like Nadya," Malcolm said.

Dr. Brenner grinned, his face a mass of wrinkles. "So long! I'll drop in tonight again, if I don't hear from you."

"Thanks," Malcolm said.

He went downstairs after the doctor was gone and sat directly beneath Nadya's room, to listen if she called. But she did not call and the baby did not cry. Leora made him some lunch and he ate it. She washed up and went home and he read the hours away. Three times he climbed the stairs and opened the door and looked in. It was afternoon before Nadya woke and even then only because Peter and Lise came home.

"Hush," he told them when they came impetuously into the house. "We have a baby—a boy."

They stopped, uncertain for an instant what to do. They knew—oh, of course they knew, they had all talked together about Thomas, and even about Lucie, who would be born next year. But this was home talk and outside neither had told anyone of the expected birth. It was a little shameful outside for people as old as their parents to have a baby. Here at home it was all right because they behaved as though the baby was already part of the family. But outside people would surely laugh, and laughter was what Peter and Lise feared above all else. That their parents were different they could not deny and they knew themselves different, however well they prepared the surface of their likeness to others of their own age. Now, however, their natural goodness overcame them.

"Where is he?" Lise whispered.

Peter yielded suddenly, too, and raced up the stairs. Malcolm repressed his impulse to shout after them. Nadya had slept long enough to be refreshed. He would not rob her of the joy of showing her children their baby brother. He climbed the stairs smiling and went into the room. Nadya was leaning on her elbow, watching her children, her heavy blond braid dropping over her shoulder. Lise had lifted Thomas from his crib, wrapped in his blue blanket, and she was looking down at his sleeping face. Tenderness and dawning curiosity were in her vivid face, and Peter stood beside her, his angular young face doubting, half embarrassed.

"Our three children," Nadya said. Her voice broke, and the ready tears rushed to her eyes.

This moment, jeweled in his memory, shone forth a month later when he stood before his first American audience, although there was no connection between that vivid scene in a bedroom in his own house, when he stood gazing at his family, and this moment when, a stranger, he stood before a hall filled with strangers. Yet the same powerful feeling of reality rushed over him and waked him to intense awareness. Life leaped from one such moment to another, each with its own meaning, vivid, strong, and raw, the moments connected by long subdued intervals, a membrane of days and nights made of the routines of food and sleep and work and the necessities implied. Yet suddenly, one never knew on what day or at what hour, the sharp awareness of a scene and the people in it lifted mind and heart to intensity again.

Thus there was relation between the warm center now hundreds of miles away, where Nadya and the children lived and waited for his return, and this bare hall in a midwestern state, filled tonight with people he did not know. He did not know them, and to them he was a name of no interest, even as a name, except that he had lived in a strange land in which, too, they had no interest except that there was now the fear of war and personal involvement, their sons and husbands possibly having to leave the shelter of homes in the towns and on the farms to go away across the sea, perhaps to die. This fear and this fear alone caught them and made them look up to him with dubious expectancy as he stood on the platform behind a tall narrow podium, his hands gripping its sides as he stared straight down into the mass of upturned faces, white in the dimness of the hall lights.

This was his chance, this was his mission. He would tell them first of all why it was that the world had come to its present pass, how step by step through hundreds of years the Western peoples had moved in upon Asia, through trade and government and religion, and how the message of these mighty ones had been preached and taught by example and by force and was now bearing fruit, in confusion, it was true, in waste and in war, but these were superficial. Deep in the heart of Asia something new was stirring, something good or evil but certainly not to be feared if it were faced and understood.

He stood for a moment in silence, yearning over these, his own people who, though strangers to him, were closer to him than all the world besides. Then he began to speak in a clear voice, choosing simple words in which to clothe the vastness of his thought. "To-night I bring you good news. We have the choice between war and peace. We are not compelled. We are men and women of free will. If we have the patience to learn the truths which lead to peace, we shall have peace. I know you yearn for the certainty of peace, as I do, also. We have built our homes, our sons and our daughters are born, we long to nurture them in safety. Life is meant for our benefit and our enjoyment, and not for our destruction. I bring you the good news that destruction is not inevitable, if we do not destroy ourselves——"

He spoke for an hour, outlining in strong strokes the march of history to the present hour, making them see, oh, surely they did see, that there was always the choice of war or peace. The choice was possible until the final bomb fell, the bomb that must never fall.

They listened. He knew for the first time the intoxication of hundreds of people listening in silence and close attention. This was better than the writing of books, this was the direct way, the swift communication. He felt strong currents flowing from his mind to theirs. He was honest with them, he told them that which he knew absolutely, the places where he had been, the people whose faces he had seen on the other side of the world and whose languages he spoke.

"I know," he said, "because I have been there. These are facts."

He closed at the end of an hour, and when he sat down there was silence and then approval burst from them in roars of applause. They wanted to believe him, they did believe him. He sat quietly, hearing the sound of their clapping hands, feeling that what he had done was good.

The chairman, who was the mayor of the town, a brisk, robust, red-haired man, got to his feet and stammered his thanks. "And now," he said, "Mr. MacNeil will answer your questions. I am sure that this stimulating address will make you want to ask him a lot of questions."

No one did ask questions, not for a long minute and then another and yet another. Malcolm lifted his head and gazed over at the motionless people. No questions! Yes, there was one. A man got up in the front seat, a young man, heavy-set, his blond hair too long. He wore no coat and he had rolled up the sleeves of his blue shirt.

Malcolm rose and went again to the podium to receive the question. "Yes?"

The young man drawled and halted. "I couldn' foller eve'ything you said, mister, not eve'ything, that is. But it sounded mighty complex to me, mighty complex. Wouldn't it be a whole lot simpler just to drop some atomic bombs on the whole Commy outfit?"

He looked around, grinning, and snickers rose here and there. Someone hissed, someone laughed.

Malcolm felt himself seized by rage. He controlled himself. "This is not, in my opinion, a serious question."

"Sure," the young man insisted. "I mean it serious."

Malcolm stared down at the sneering blond face and compelled his voice to quiet. "If all that I have said does not answer your question, then I doubt that you can be convinced by anything except bombs. Is there another question?"

There was none. The meeting had suddenly divided itself. Malcolm was on one side and the blond young man on the other. No one wanted to take sides openly and the red-haired mayor closed the meeting abruptly.

Polite words, leave-taking, a few people came up to shake his hand and to murmur thanks, timid thanks, but the people who had listened to him raptly, as he thought, went plodding home again, and he went back to his hotel room, crestfallen, bewildered, all his exaltation gone. What had happened? People could not listen with all their hearts, their eyes fixed on his face, the hall silent, their very breathing subdued, and then go home again as they had come. What did they think of what he had said? Did they approve or disapprove? He could not answer his own questions, and he went upstairs to the dingy room, lonely as he had never been lonely in his whole life. To speak as he had done, out of profound experience, with all the keenness of mind and heart awakened, and then to get no response! What was the matter with his people? He sat down to ponder, and his thoughts began to center themselves upon the blond young man. That man was the key to the puzzle. He was someone in this town. When the fellow asked his question, that stupid, ignorant, absurd question, as dangerous and blind as the bomb itself, then no one dared to speak. *But what did it mean that no one dared?*

The telephone rang and he lifted the receiver. He heard a voice, familiar and yet which he could not recognize.

"MacNeil?"

"Yes—who is it?"

"Do you remember Elliott Rackman?"

Rackman! But here? "Of course I do," he said warmly. "But what are you doing here? I thought you were still in Outer Mongolia."

"I'm here teaching in a small university. I heard you tonight but I thought I'd wait until you got back to your room."

"Come on over, man! I was just sitting here, feeling rueful."

"I'll be over." The quiet voice was too quiet, almost as though Rackman were afraid. But afraid of what?

"Come straight up to the third floor, the first door on the left of the elevator," Malcolm urged.

"I'll be over," the too quiet voice said again.

In something under half an hour there was a knock at the door and Malcolm opened it. The corridors were silent, it was well past midnight, but Rackman looked left and right before he entered. He was the same slender, rather short figure that Malcolm remembered. He shut the door. "Sit down, Rackman. It's good to find a friend here. I was feeling damned lonely all of a sudden, after that speech. Did I cast pearls before swine? What was the matter?"

Elliott Rackman sat down. His movements were almost Oriental in their grace. Years ago Malcolm had come upon him in a lama temple in Tibet, wrapped in the saffron robe of a priest, living as a lama among lamas. He was burned brown with Tibetan sun, his skin the color of the dry earth, and only the startling color of his eyes, gray-green, like old buried jade, had betrayed his race.

Now, without the yellow robes, Rackman's frame was slight and inconspicuous, but his strongly marked features, black hair and small black moustache, his brown skin, and the startling eyes were still unchanged.

Malcolm said, "I didn't know you were in America. Why?"

Rackman smiled ruefully, "I suppose for the same reason that you are. I am an American, and it is a moment now when Americans ought to be at home. Besides, I love my country in a curious deep sort of way, even though I was born in China."

"I didn't know that," Malcolm said. "Somehow I had an idea you were an Englishman."

"No, my father was a missionary, one of the old school, I suppose, the sort one doesn't see any more, embattled for righteousness, and so on, in his peculiar way. When it came to a final decision, the decision we have all to make these days, it was that same righteousness that made me choose my own country, though I've never lived here, and God knows, I find it hard—impossible, except that I have a vague yearning to be of use here, in my time. The missionary reversed, I suppose! I can hear my father snort in his grave. He couldn't have imagined a missionary being needed in America. If you hadn't said what you did tonight, I wouldn't have disclosed my existence to you, MacNeil. But you see the wonderful chance we have now in the world—the chance and the danger."

The quiet of midnight lay upon the town. In their beds in the darkened houses the people were sleeping their usual sleep, undisturbed by the knowledge the two men shared.

"Have Americans a chance?" Malcolm asked.

"If they can only see it in time," Rackman replied.

They fell silent for a moment, sharing their memories of other lands and other times, the inexplicable fascination of ancient peoples simplified and made profound by centuries of human living, who face to face at last with modern thought and modern ways, doubted, were tempted and repelled, who waited for hints of friendship from Western strangers. These peoples waited against landscapes of desert and sand-bitten mountains, against opulent plains and tropic hills and valleys and monstrous rivers flowing across the continents and the whole of Asia came alive again while the two Americans faced each other, thinking and remembering.

"I feel as if men like ourselves were single-handed and without weapons," Malcolm said. "You in your college here and I tramping across the country from little town to little town! Why on earth are you stuck in a college?"

"I have to earn my living," Rackman said.

"And I mine," Malcolm replied. "I've written a book—but there'll be no living in that and I have a wife and three children."

"Thank God I am alone," Rackman said simply. "If anything happens to me, there'll be no one to suffer."

"What can happen to you?"

"Anything, depending upon the turn of events," Rackman said without apparent concern.

"That tells me nothing," Malcolm declared. "Come, you've been here longer than I—how many years?"

"I left when we gave Mongolia to Russia. I had to decide then where I belonged. Now I am not sure where I belong. Yes, I am, too! Did you take a long look at the brawny blond fellow who asked you tonight whether it wasn't better just to drop some bombs?"

"Yes, I saw him," Malcolm said.

"He's everywhere," Rackman said. "In every town and village, and Lord knows how many of him there are in the cities. He's in Washington, in the Senate, in the House, he's in the Rotary Clubs and the veterans' organizations. He's the big simple he-man, the man of action, the man who doesn't see why anyone should think. Just act, that's all!"

"Well?" Malcolm inquired.

"Nothing," Rackman said. "But did you look at the rest of them—all the quiet ones who didn't speak? And why didn't they? Because the brawny fellow who never finished high school has a gun and they don't! They have weapons but they don't know it. He takes out his gun and yells Communist. They don't know what to do. They've never been held up like this before. They don't really know what a Communist is except that at the moment it's the wrong thing to be. But are we all going to sit quiet, say nothing, hear nothing, do nothing like stone monkeys?"

Malcolm met the demand of the steadfast green-gray eyes. "I believe if our people know——"

Rackman got up, too. "There isn't time for them to know. You have a fine idealistic purpose, my lad, but there's no time for it. You'll wear yourself out but it will all be too late."

"What do you propose to do then?"

"Nothing—I've done all I can throughout these years. I've been an American wandering in the buffer land between China and Russia. I've written for newspapers, I've talked to diplomats and consuls. Now I'm writing a book. When it's written and published and has raised its hell, which it will because it is full of all the things that nobody wants to know, then we'll see what happens to me. I hope you won't feel you must come to my rescue. You can't afford it, if you have to make your living."

"You were always a pessimist," Malcolm said, smiling.

"I've been right, haven't I? I told you when the Japanese took Manchuria what would happen, didn't I? I told you in Peking, at a damned dinner dance at the embassy. And it has happened and you and I are here—refugees in our own country!" He laughed, a singularly melodious sound, soft and rich with genuine sad amusement.

He put out his hand. "Oh, well, goodbye, MacNeill We're friends, but I'll understand that there are limits nowadays to friendship."

When he was gone Malcolm felt himself shadowed

by foreboding. The little hotel room was suddenly a prison. There stood the narrow hotel bed, covered with its cheap blankets and washable cover and he had no longing to sleep in it. He put on his topcoat and went outside instead, into the darkness barely lit by a few streetlamps. Not a soul was to be seen. He could imagine himself the only man in a deserted town. The sky showed neither moon nor stars and he saw no lighted house. Yet somewhere in those closed houses slept the silent people and the brawny fool.

He left on the early morning train and the endless pattern of America unfolded itself as he traveled on. The journey swept in an enormous ellipse, northwest, south and southeast. The landscape changed and changed again, mountains and deserts, valleys and rivers, cliffs, torrents, and immense flat plains, motionless except for the wind upon the long grass, but the people did not change. In a strange and common unity they ate the same foods, lived in houses large or small but the same houses, infinite in variety and yet alike, speaking the same language, infinite again in variety of tone and enunciation, but the same language, embodying the same thoughts, expressing the same interests, few indeed, he thought sorrowfully, and the world was not their concern. They wore the world like a garment too new and too large for them and they sought to cast it off and draw about themselves the safe old coat they knew, too small and sorely outgrown, and this, too, they did not know.

Night after night he spoke to the same sea of upturned faces. white in the darkness and seldom indeed did he see before him any but the white faces, though on the streets by day, walking unknown and alone, he saw Mexican faces and Indian faces and again and again the Negroes, but these did not come to hear him and he did not know them. He was not sure that he changed the thinking of any mind behind the faces, but he himself was changed. He became urgent and pleading, what Rackman had said was true, there was no time left now for teaching. He must plead and warn and threaten and yet always he ended with hope.

"If we Americans can see and understand that this is our opportunity, God given, I believe, to prove our ways and our thoughts to all men, then through us will come the golden age of mankind."

This was his unvarying peroration, and the people sat motionless, stirred, however vaguely, by the gates he threw open before them. They applauded and then they moved in their seats, they thought of home and bed and sleep, and the next day's work. They rose and fumbled for their hats and coats, they stumbled out again into the night and a man said to his wife, "Want a soda?" And she said, "I don't care if I do." And so what he had said faded away. Who cares for the golden streets of heaven?

And over and over again he found the same brawny fool ready to spout his question, which was no question but the argument of unanswerable ignorance and stupidity: "We'd better drop the bomb and be done with it." The Bomb was God, in whom fools trusted.

Somewhere in the southwest, somewhere in the south, somewhere—he forgot the towns as soon as he had left them—he came upon American missionaries whom he had met in China when he was their consul and missionaries he had never met but they were all the same. They were home again, and whatever seed they had sown upon those far fields was now plowed under and cast away. They were bewildered and for that he felt sorry for them. Their sad eyes confessed that God had not stood by them, they were betrayed, their pleasant service ended. Or they were confident that the seed, sown so thinly, would still bear fruit, "in God's time," they told him with brave, bright faith. He felt sorry for them, too. God's time? But God's time was yesterday, today, and forever. And how the brawny fools laughed at the missionaries! A lot of money wasted on heathen foreigners! The Bomb, the Bomb was the Thing, and the Thing was God. And the people were silent, wherever he went.

He reached home in November, in time for Thanksgiving, and on the eastward journey home, his destination, became first a necessity and then a flight. Money was in his pocket, it had been a successful tour, his agent said, well worth repeating, but he knew that it was a failure. There were other ways to make money and he need not make it by the destruction of his soul. For he would be destroyed if he returned again and again to the towns and the cities to meet the same white faces, unmoving in the twilight of the halls where he saw himself standing solitary, his voice ringing out against silence, his earnest determination beating against indifference. It was amiable, he was convinced of that, it was childlike in its easy kindness to him, as a human being. It was the strange quality of Americans, that they could be familiar and easy and kind, nearly always very kind, and yet beyond it was callous indifference. He felt bruised and bewildered, deceived by the surface kindness, crushed by the inner hardness of his own people. Was it merely ignorance of the world? If so, then what was its quality, that it was harder than the marble hills?

He was exhausted, spent, emptied of all the inner richness with which he had begun his journey. There was nothing left in him except the desire for home, and for the few human beings who were his own. He avoided his sisters, although he passed within a few miles of their two houses and although it had been his plan to stop and visit them. Instead he went straight as an eagle to its nest, and arrived at the small and dingy railroad station early one morning.

He would in other times have been touched by the ready greeting of the station master, unshaven and perennially in gartered shirtsleeves, but he had been greeted thus too often and this amiability was the same cover for the inner hardness he now suspected everywhere.

"Hiya, Mister MacNeil, nice to see you back! I saw Mrs. MacNeil yesterday. She was on her way to the store, I reckon. She was lookin' handsome."

"It's good to be home," Malcolm said.

"Nobody here to meet you, is there?" the station master went on. "You want to telephone home or shall I call Horace?"

"I believe I'll surprise my family and let Horace drive me," he said.

"Okay. It won't be more than a few minutes. Horace won't be gone yet——"

He sat down on the slatted bench in the waiting room and gave way to weariness. It was more than physical. He needed an inner reconstruction. His spirit was eaten away, disillusioned, perhaps, and yet he was not willing to be disillusioned by his own people. Somewhere his own understanding of them had failed. His approach had presumed too much. They knew less than he had thought they did. To get home, to live with Nadya again and be with his children and restore himself was his first necessity, to rest and then to think, perhaps to try again, or never try again.

"Horace is here, Mr. MacNeil."

"All right and thanks." He got to his feet and, carrying his bags, he went outside and climbed into the old Ford car, driven by Horace, an immense fat man, whose German ancestors lived again in his thick and stubborn frame.

"Well, you been away," Horace observed.

"Nearly three months," Malcolm said.

"Yeah," Horace said.

He started the car with a frightful roar and a rush of dust and they rattled along the seventeen miles to the bridge. Beyond it Malcolm could see his house set on the hillside. It looked tranquil, a patient edifice of stone, sheltering generation after generation of men and women and their children. The black walnut tree was bare but the last bright leaves still clung to the maples, and over the woods an opalescent tinge of fading rose and brown hung like a mist.

He gazed at the scene and felt a sentimental warmth that was new to him. Here was something his own, here he could live and work with freedom, whatever was outside.

I'll never leave it again, he thought grimly.

Horace was the wise one, who never wandered a mile from his beaten road, and cared not enough even to ask a question of what lay beyond. Not once in the seventeen miles had he asked where Malcolm had been or what he had seen, and reflecting upon this unconcern, it occurred to Malcolm that no one in his entire journey asked anything about Peking or the life beyond the ocean, not even Corinne or Susanna had asked so much as a casual question. "But what did you have to eat over there, Malcolm?" or "Did you sleep on beds like ours, and were the houses the same?" There were no questions, and this, too, was a kind of silence. When in other years he had traveled about China, stopping at villages or in towns, the people had besieged him with their curiosity, they had tortured him with questions, scarcely leaving him time to sleep or dress in privacy. Their lively minds had wanted to know everything about another country. They had even asked him whether foreigners had children in the same fashion that Chinese did.

"We hear," a dignified old village elder had told him, "that your women give birth through a hole cut in the belly."

Why should he think of that old village elder now, as he sat behind Horace's vast back? Except that had this wreck of a Ford been on a Chinese road, dusty and corded with ruts, the driver would have risked their lives by wanting to know all about him, his ancestors, and his country. Silence would have been impossible.

It was pleasant just now, however, to approach the house. The day was still early enough to hope that the children had not gone to school. He got out of the cab and paid Horace before they saw him. Then the doors opened and Nadya came running out, with Peter and Lise racing behind. He had an impression of clean, gaily colored garments, Nadya in blue, Lise in striped red and white something, and Peter's shirt was yellow, and these bright colors against flying blond hair and blue eyes and pink cheeks. Nadya flung herself into his arms, the tears running down her laughing face.

"Oh, Malcolm, my darling, my darling—so terrible it has been—don't go any more, Malcolm, please——"

"No——"

He held her in a long embrace, while the children waited. Then Lise squeezed herself between them, and Malcolm reached out and drew Peter in with his right arm.

"Oh heaven," Nadya exclaimed. "Thomas! We forget him!"

She rushed away again upstairs, and took Thomas from his crib where he lay sleeping in his morning nap, and brought him down in his blue flannel nightgown.

"What!" Malcolm exclaimed in proper astonishment. "This monster is Thomas?"

The child was large and fat, and totally changed from the little creature he had seen born. He was a placid child and he stared at his father with surprise.

"Ah, Thomas," Nadya cried, "you must not look surprise at your father! Malcolm, I have showed him every day your picture but still he is not sure who you are. Shameful child!"

"Mamá, you are too silly," Lise said passionately. "He's only a baby."

She snatched Thomas away and cradled him against her shoulder and walked with him indignantly into the house. Nadya laughed. "He is Lise's baby, it is only I who bore him and wash his clothes."

"Peter is changed," Malcolm said to his son. His right arm lay on his son's shoulder and they walked together to the house.

"Taller," Peter said.

"Changed," Malcolm repeated. He looked at Nadya and caught a look on her face which was inexplicable, a little afraid, or perhaps only pleading, lips pressed together, eyes wistfully on Peter, who did not look at her.

"He is changed," she said. "It is something you must talk with your father, Peter. I am not able to know what to do. After all, it is new to be here and perhaps I do not give good advice. About other countries, yes, but not yet America! But we will have breakfast first, Malcolm. You are hungry, I am sure."

"And tired and dusty," he said.

"Wash, eat, sleep," she directed. "Peter and Lise must go to school meanwhile."

He yielded too willingly, perhaps, for there was a look of reserve on his son's face that meant something. While he had been away Peter doubtless had been learning, too. Perhaps the way to learn was to stay in one place and go deep.

"Peter and Lise, eat your breakfast and hurry away to school," Nadya said. "This afternoon your papá will spend with you when you come home. Now there is no time."

She hastened them gaily, her blue eyes sparkling, her fair hair electric, and all her being incandescent with joy. Love shone from her like a light, and when they were upstairs alone, she went into his arms again, murmuring. "Oh, Malcolm, to leave me so long! I want to be alone with you—I want them to go to school and I shall give Leora a holiday, the day off, how she calls it. Let us be alone, my love!"

It was she who was articulate, as she had always been, and he had never learned to pour out his love in abundant words, but he had his own ways. He kissed her again and again, and tumbled her blond head in his hand, growling, she said, like a bear, and she was happy, happy, only he must not go away again, never so long.

Then, Thomas, thoroughly awakened, shouted for food, and they tore themselves apart, she to nurse the child at her full breast and Malcolm to bathe and change and when he went downstairs, Leora was already gone, and Nadya was making him the breakfast he liked best.

"Such hen's eggs," she said proudly, "our own, Malcolm, and like nothing tasted before. And I do have the cows now milking, ten cows, please, and a young farmer to help me. So much, so much to show you! I make the butter, see how yellow it is! I made it fresh yesterday. At least the cows and chickens you must see, Malcolm, before you sleep."

She fed him lavishly, bacon and eggs, and her baked bread and coffee as only she could make coffee with

her Russian brewing and now the rich fresh cream. He
was amazed at her.

"I always knew you could do everything, my wife,
but this is certainly new to me. I never saw you a
farmer, Nadya."

"I have done many things," she said in the same
proud way. "In Harbin we had always a little garden,
some chickens, and a yellow cow. My father did not
touch them, but we had to eat, and it is the woman's
business to make food somehow, my mother always
did say, and so we did it. Of course in Peking it was
not necessary, the Chinese are too clever, and we were
there only ladies again."

She laughed and reached her two hands across the
table and put her palms on his cheeks and said in Russian, "Ah, Malcolm, to see thy face again!"

When they had eaten they washed the dishes together and then hand in hand they went upstairs to
perform the rite of bath for Thomas. He sat idle, watching her swift compact movements, and then she handed
him the clean and naked child to admire.

"He is amazing, is he not, Malcolm? Look at his
shoulders and those fat thighs, and such big hands and
feet, hasn't he? Will he be truly American, do you
think? Is he not too Russian to see?"

"He'll be American," Malcolm said, "but not a big
blond brawny brute. That I will not allow."

He sat his son on his knees and upheld him by his
hands under the child's arms, and he gazed into the
inquiring baby eyes. Thomas stared at his father without wavering, motionless, curious, asking. The question
was not so much who are you, not so specific as that,
but one far more profound: "What is this new world?"

"I don't know, my son," Malcolm muttered. "I'm
facing it myself."

The house was shelter and comfort and safety. It was a deep reserve of human love, Nadya the center and the source, and in her radiance they basked and love grew in manifold life, the love of man and woman between him and Nadya, and their love for each individual child, the tender, half-humorous love he had for Lise, his daughter, different indeed from Nadya's rich and sometimes exacting woman-love for her daughter, and his love, half-stern, half-tender, for Peter, his son, different again from Nadya's love for her son, tender and admiring and sensitive to the man he was to be, and their whole love for the small Thomas, as yet content merely to let him be what he was, and the responding love of the children, Lise and Peter so different, for the parents and for each other. But it was all love, and Malcolm felt the waves of love around him, and for a few days he did nothing except small things outdoors in the barn and garden, the last rites of autumn dying into winter. He chopped wood for the fireplaces and he gathered leaves and mulched the flower beds and the vegetable garden against the coming cold and he listened to the advice of old Yarcy, by now the master, in his own opinion, of the place and these strange people to whom it belonged, even advising the young farmer, Joseph, and although Yarcy knew nothing about cows, he was full of advice on breeding and calving and feed.

Nadya had contrived in the months she had been alone to create in the farm a bursting center of life, the half dozen cows in the barn lowed as though they had always been there, and Joseph, dogged and noncommittal, a low-browed, round-faced yokel of a man, was no more than a boy, but at eighteen married to a stupid, pretty, seventeen-year-old girl who was already pregnant.

"A shotgun wedding," old Yarcy whispered to Malcolm out of the side of his Saturday quid. "You'd think a feller 'at worked on a farm would know what happens, hey?"

He cackled laughter and winked his drooping right eyelid.

But Nadya liked Joseph, she said she understood him, and though he doubted often that she was right in her commands, for she read a thick book and then told him what to do, and whoever heard of farmin' out of a book? Nevertheless he did what she said, and the cows was milkin' good. He was glad for a job, for his family and his wife's family had been upset over the wedding and the baby coming too soon after, not for decency's sake but because it meant three mouths to feed.

"You git out and make your own livin'," his father had ordered and Joseph had got out, taking courage to go next door to the "foreigners" and ask for a job. Nadya had taken him on the spot.

"He looks like a good muzhik," she told Malcolm.

Nadya was happy, he believed. She was constantly busy, and if her acquaintances were still only the grocer and his wife, the postmistress and the children's schoolteachers and the clerks in the small general store, she was happy, or so he thought, watching her make the enormous round loaves of bread, watching her bustle to keep the house clean and bathe Thomas and put him to sleep in his carriage outside in the sun, watching her put up hearty lunches for Lise and Peter to take to school, and dash out between times to barn or yard, scolding old Yarcy while she laughed at him and met his arguments head on.

"Oh, Yarcy, you are so funny, just like old Russian!"

"Now don't you call me no names!" Yarcy protested, grinning.

"You're happy, aren't you, Nadya?" Malcolm said one

morning when he came into the kitchen for his breakfast.

"Oh, entire," she exclaimed with enthusiasm. "I am washing the dishes and Leora makes the beds and cleans upstairs."

He sat down at the small table by the window, half ashamed at the lateness of the hour, but he had worked late last night in his study, planning a new book. This one would be entirely different, something far more elementary. His first book, due to be published just after the first of the year, he now dreaded to think about. He had written it without knowing his own people and it would fail, he was sure. He had taken too much for granted, a primary knowledge of the world and of human history, especially in Asia, which he knew did not exist among Americans. In this book he would take nothing for granted.

Nadya turned an egg neatly in the pan where she had fried bacon. "Almost I am happy entirely," she amended.

"Why almost?" he demanded.

She poured coffee into his cup. "Do you not see something wrong about Peter?"

"Is there something wrong?"

"Perhaps I am wrong."

"Don't be Russian with me," he protested. "Don't talk in circles."

She sat down in the chair opposite him, put bread into the toaster, and poured herself a cup of coffee. "Peter was in some trouble while you went away."

"Trouble? You didn't tell me."

"I think you are tired, so I didn't tell you. Now perhaps better that I do tell you. Malcolm, it is like this. He came home from school one day saying that in his class, and I don't know why in school they talk such things at all, that a teacher said the Chinese Communists have done something very torturous to American prisoners, something of atrocity, in other words, and Peter said perhaps it is true but in war all soldiers are sometimes torturous, and then he told how it was in China during the war with Japan, that Americans also did some atrocities. He was innocently talking, wanting only to tell the truth, and you know, Malcolm, our children will always love the Chinese, it is impossible otherwise, remembering Peking and our house there and the friends we had, Chinese. So then the teacher denied Peter this truth, and she said that Americans are never doing atrocities, this is impossible, she said, and then Peter got angry for the sake of the truth and he told what did happen in China from some Americans, not all, but some, and you know, Malcolm, we did see ourselves how that blond young American, only nineteen, so tall and beautiful looking, how with his gun stock he broke the skulls of the living Japanese prisoners lying on the ground——"

"Don't," Malcolm said. "Let's not remember that."

It was true. He had seen it himself one night on a battlefield in the last war. A tall fair-haired American, a man with a child's face, had suddenly gone mad with rage at the sight of a row of Japanese prisoners, living men, who lay on the ground, tied hand and foot ready to be taken away in a truck to a prisoners' camp. The fair-haired man had lifted his gun, and bringing it stock down with all his young strength, he had mashed in the faces of the captive Japanese. He had crushed their skulls, and he had not been punished.

And there was the story that a Chinese general had told of the opening of hatches in airplanes over the Himalayas—but this, too, was not to be remembered and never to be told.

"There is no use in repeating atrocities," he said sternly. "Peter ought to know better than that."

"He was not thinking of atrocities but of truth," Nadya cried passionately. "We have taught him to love the truth, Malcolm, and so all that he said was what he has heard us say—that in any war men on both sides can do such strange and wicked things, and it is not the truth to say it comes all on one side, but when he said this, the teacher called him a Communist, and even did say to him that his mother is Russian—I, Malcolm, to have a son who could be anything Communist when all my family was destroyed by them and my life spent as a refugee, and my old parents dying and being buried in a strange land!"

She began to weep, wiping her eyes on the table napkin, and he reached across the little table and took her face in his hands.

"My dear," he said, "please don't cry! You have been alone too long. I will talk with Peter. I will set the troubles right."

The trouble was not mentioned until the evening was there before them. They had eaten a hearty supper of borscht and dark bread and thin-sliced chicken, Nadya's chicken stuffed with onions and roasted, and a bowl of tossed green salad. Thomas had been admired and played with and put to bed and Lise set firmly on the path of arithmetic and in her own room.

Then Nadya said, "Peter, you will please explain to your father the disagreement between us. He will solve it for us."

Peter halted on the stairs with his books, a too tall, delicate-looking boy, sprouting soft hair on his face and arms. "Mamá, I have a lot of homework to do tonight. Besides——"

"Come," Nadya said firmly. "This morning I cried and your father said he would help us."

"We'll watch the clock, Peter," Malcolm said.

Peter came back reluctantly and with the permanent, subdued revolt of the adolescent upon his face, he sat down wordless and holding his books in his arms ostentatiously.

"Put the books down on the floor," Malcolm said. "We will forget them for the moment."

"Tomorrow is coming," Peter said stubbornly.

Malcolm ignored this, and Nadya sat down and clasped her hands lightly on her lap. But Peter remained silent and to diminish the weight of this silence between them, Malcolm began to talk.

"We are all trying to understand our own country, Peter, where we are strangers actually. We are each trying at our own luck, you with the boys of your age, Lise with girls, your mother is making a home for us in ways which she has not had to do before, without servants, for certainly Leora is nothing like the servants we had in Peking and indeed she is not a servant at all. I don't know what she is—a helper of sorts, perhaps."

"A young girl dreaming," Nadya put in.

"Perhaps! And I am, in a way, as much of a dreamer, I suppose. I went on my lecture tour, Peter, with an idea that all I had to do was to explain the meaning of history to my own people, whom I thought I understood because I grew up here. After all, I am born an American. I have come back realizing that history and facts mean nothing here. To our people everything is a matter of feeling and emotion, a curious mixed sort of idealism that is powerful because in some ways it is very sound. But it is unrelated to the facts of the world. The problem is much more severe than I thought. People cannot learn by hearing, because there is no foundation of knowledge. They do not read history. They read only newspapers, which deal with today's events, but these events are the result of yesterday's events and it is necessary to know those which come first."

He forgot that his son was still too young to be concerned with history.

He was talking as he might have talked to an audience. Nadya listened respectfully, admiring him and agreeing with him as a matter of course.

Malcolm laughed suddenly and uncomfortably. "Excuse me, Peter——"

He was touched and then moved beyond proportion when Peter put down his books on the floor and gazed at him with interest. "Go on, Papá," he said. "Nobody has told me this before."

But Malcolm could not go on. "Perhaps that is all, Peter, except that you must remember everything has its cause."

"Papá," Peter said intensely, "I want to ask you something."

"Yes, my son?"

"Do I keep silent when I hear someone say a thing which I know is not true? As, for example, when Miss Roderick says that the Chinese are torturing the prisoners they take from our side, not because the Chinese are Communists, Papá, but because they are Chinese and just now our enemies. Papá, am I not to speak the truth?"

"Oh," Nadya sighed, "this is the whole question!"

Malcolm felt himself nailed to a cross by his own son. With all his heart he believed in the beauty of truth, with his mind he believed in its necessity—else how could man continue to live honorably with mankind upon this little globe? And yet, if he said to his son, "Speak the truth at whatever cost," what today might be the monstrous cost? It occurred to him while he hesitated that everywhere men and women looked at their children as he was looking at Peter, who waited, and he began to understand something of the reason for their silence.

He got up from his chair and walked to the window and looked out over the rolling wooded hills and the valleys between, lying neatly in fields of sprouting winter wheat. The clear, cold moonlight fell upon this landscape, subduing color and carving out in black and silver the outlines and the shadows. A peaceful scene, he would have said, and yet he knew that in no household where there were parents and children could there be peace. For at this hour parents must choose between debauching their children, telling them to deny truth to save their skins, or telling them to speak the truth, when the cost might be death. Yes, it might be death. He thought of Rackman, living surely a precarious life, liable at any moment to dismissal from his job. For a young man uncertainty was no better than death. A small question, he might have told Peter, a local incident, easy enough to ignore, but he knew that it was no small question. If he said, "My son, keep silent, for safety's sake," these words would destroy Peter's soul.

"Oh," Nadya cried, "if we could only live! Let us just live together and love each other, my darlings! Let us not think of anything except to live here in our home."

Neither answered her, not husband, not son, and she bowed her head on her knees and sobbed twice and then she jumped up from her chair and ran out of the room, still sobbing.

When the door shut, Malcolm turned and stood before his son. "The only way I know is honesty, and so I have to say that I cannot tell you what to do. No father can tell his son today what to do. Your generation is faced with problems that we never knew. I can only say that I myself must live by what I believe. I shall continue to tell the truth as I know it. But this may not be the truth you know. And certainly the consequences of truth are more severe for you than for me. I have no right to advise."

Peter's lips trembled, but no tears came to his eyes. He had learned to weep no more. Instead, he stooped and picked up the heap of tumbled books from the floor and piled them neatly on his knees. Then he put them under his arm and stood up.

"Thank you, Papá," he said in his usual voice. "And now I'd better do my homework."

He walked out of the room, his slender body leaning to balance the books, and Malcolm stood watching him and knew for the first time in his life the whole agony of parenthood.

Epilogue
For
Today

THERE HAVE BEEN TIMES in my life when I have written books and left them uncompleted, and this for various reasons. Perhaps the characters have developed beyond me, so that I must live longer in order to understand them more fully. Perhaps I need further growth within myself. Perhaps I come to the decision that the book does not suit the times in which I live, or perhaps my country or my people. Then I lay the unfinished work aside, to be brought to the right conclusion at the right time.

I never forget these books entirely. No, that is not quite true, for I do put them out of my mind, sometimes for days, sometimes for weeks, even for years. Then, inexplicably, the right time appears, it may be in a moment, or it may grow slowly out of widening experience. So it has been with this book, *All Under Heaven,* or as the Chinese would say it, *"P'u T'ien Tse Hsia."*

The phrase, by the way, is a classical one from ancient Chinese literature and is probably not known to the young Chinese who at this moment are not studying the classics. It is followed in full quotation by two other words, "*wei gung*," which complete the meaning to be "All Under Heaven Are One." But truth remains eternal, whatever our times, and so I repeat it.

I do not know why I took out this unfinished, incomplete book recently and decided to finish it. Yes, I *do* know. It is because we have begun a new era. We are in communication again with my other country, China. Oh, what changes have taken place since I left it so many years ago to come home to the land of my ancestors, my own country, the United States of America! Will the Chinese people understand us? And will we, can we, understand them? Their history is so long, ours so short, they are so old, we are so young. Can there be understanding when there is such difference? There *must* be, it is essential, not only for our own two countries, but for the peace of the whole world.

And, thinking these troubled thoughts one day a few months ago, I felt a familiar alarm, always deep within me, rise up again, but just now in the shape of a man. I remembered a character of my own creation whom I had put aside in an unfinished novel. I did not know then, years ago, how to complete that novel. I did not even know what to title it. Suddenly Malcolm's face, his form, rose clear in my memory, his question then my question today. But today, Malcolm, I know how to finish the book. Now I have finished it. These are the last pages, this page the final words. Only two days ago I wondered how to title it. By luck—no, nothing is by luck—the title came floating into my mind *All Under Heaven*—ancient words, forever true! But will my people understand? Yes, now I believe they will understand. We have grown very fast, even in these last few weeks. And again by chance that is not chance, an old Chinese friend was visiting me and in his fine Chinese script he wrote the words for me, *All Under Heaven:*

Yes, the title is incomplete. It does not go on to say "are one." Not yet! I leave it incomplete because that is the way it is. I am only a solitary woman, sitting lonely at her desk. Peoples Under Heaven, I can but give you this book. It is for you to complete the title with all its meaning.

March 27, 1972
Danby House
Danby, Vermont
U. S. A.